Floxham Island
Sinclair V-log AZ267/M

by Merita King

Published by Merita King
Eastleigh
Hampshire
United Kingdom
© Merita King 2013 all rights reserved

Cover art by J L Stratton. Copyright 2013

Floxham Island ~ Sinclair V-log AZ267/M

ISBN 978-0-9570520-5-5

OTHER WORKS BY MERITA KING

The Lilean Chronicles: Book One ~ Redemption
The Lilean Chronicles: Book Two ~ The Sleeping
The Lilean Chronicles: Book Three ~ Changing Faces
The Lilean Chronicles: Book Four ~ Avalanche Effect

ABOUT THE AUTHOR

Merita King has loved the science fiction and fantasy genre in both books and movies since she was a young child. She has been greatly inspired by years of watching movies and reading books and has wanted to make a contribution to this genre for many years. Her stories all contain a strong spiritual thread as she believes that spirituality is universal and crosses all boundaries. She believes that the creative process is largely intuitive and can be very effectively blocked by too much pre-planning. "Plot lines, characters and events all come to me intuitively," she says, "and this makes the act of writing a constant pleasure." She is a psychic medium and lives alone in Hampshire, UK.

DEDICATION

For Swan, for your encouragement, assistance
and for being proud of me.

DEDICATION

INTRODUCTION

Hi there, my name is Sam Sinclair and I thought I should explain a little about what follows and tell you a little about myself. I'm a Freelance Law Enforcer, which means it's my job to catch and restrain those wanted in connection with crimes; escaped prisoners, rescue kidnap victims and that sort of thing. I used to work for the Intergalactic Law Enforcement Agency behind a desk back home on Sigma Prime but after several years I got bored and decided to go freelance. My contacts in the Law Enforcement Agency give me my jobs and so long as I get the right guy and deliver him to the right authorities, I make my own rules which suits me just fine.

There are many others out there trying to do the same job as me who aren't recognised by the Law Enforcement Agency and they're known as Mercs. Mercs just want the payout and they don't give a damn whether they have the right guy or not and they don't mind killing them to bring them in. It's even been known for them to bring in an innocent guy who just happened to look like the wanted guy, claim the payout and then make a run for it before the Agency officials found out. I hate Mercs; everybody hates Mercs but most folks tend to lump all us freelancers into the same heap under that same distasteful label.

I'm not a detective as such. My job is to find a particular person, restrain them and deliver them, not to find out if they're guilty or not nor work out why they did what they did. Over the years I've been doing this job I've met some mighty weird people and had some very strange experiences and I thought it would be cool to keep a video log of the more memorable of these encounters. I have this notion that when I retire I might release them up onto the Intergalactic Comm Web and you never know, they may even end up as Vidicom movies.

Anyway, I thought I'd test one or two out on a select few first just so I can get used to using the video uplink system and get comfortable with telling my story in my own words; it's a bit surreal sitting here talking to myself and even more so watching it back. Man do I really sound like that?

Welcome to The Sinclair V-logs, I hope you enjoy them.

CHAPTER ONE

Hang on a second while I try to fix this vidicom. There we go, that should do it. Okay this is V-log reference AZ267/M, data log reference point 2458712/6540.

Well how did it all start? A contact of mine in the Agrillian system gave me the heads up concerning a suspect they wanted to question in connection with nine murders. It took place on Agrillia 3, on an archaeological dig where a team of scientists were looking into some ancient civilisation that once inhabited that region of the planet. There were ten in the team who lived and worked at the dig for three months, after which they were due to be transported back to draw up their conclusions and official report of their findings. When the pick up got there to take them out, they found nine dead and one missing. The official law enforcement file says the usual crap; an extensive search of the locale was made etc, the suspect wasn't found etc, you know the kind of shit they come out with when they don't want to admit they were too stupid to find the guy. My contact there is a good friend so he called me up and told me about it and said would I be interested in the job and the substantial reward? Would I be interested? Hell yeah, that's my job and the promise of a substantial payout is always of interest.

The suspect they were after was some brainiac called Professor Kluvak Nembier, a native of Agrillia and up until that time he seemed to be your average well respected humourless clever guy. He had no previous record, worked hard all his life and was respected by everyone in his field of expertise, which was ancient Agrillian languages. He was one of those guys who is all brain and no brawn y'know? A guy like that is clever but seldom resourceful and tends not to be too successful at being on the run and keeping himself hidden. Having been doing this job for a long time, it was reasonable to assume that this would be one of the easiest paydays I'd had in years, so when my contact asked me if I wanted the job, I almost bit off his arm. How wrong can you be?

It took me all of two days to find out the guy had taken off and signed up as casual labour on a low budget, long haul, passenger liner that just happened to stop by Agrillia 3 at the very time he went missing. One of the whores who works the Agrillian Space Terminal remembered approaching him and being given the brush off by him. Between you and me, he was an idiot to turn her down; she is an expert in her craft, but I digress. A couple of calls told me that there was only one cruise line that called on Agrillia around that time, so after securing the details of their course I set off after them and caught up with the liner within a few days. Experience convinced me that I'd have the guy in custody within a few hours and would be able to deliver him, claim my pay check and head back to Agrillia to revisit my new lady friend at the Space Terminal to continue our umm, conversation. Boy if only I'd known then what was to come.

Being ex law enforcement myself often helps when trying to encourage folks to be co-operative and although all freelance law enforcers have to be registered, I used to be a Law Enforcement Officer myself a few years back. This means that not only do I carry the usual freelancer's ID papers but I also have the added advantage of being able to provide them with a tag. This document proves that I'm known to the Galactic Law Enforcement Agency as a trustworthy person to do business with. Being able to flash a tag is second only to flashing your official enforcer's badge and people are more likely trust you and do as you ask, which comes in mighty handy at times. There are, of course, many unregistered people trying to do this job without being officially recognised as doing so. They're universally known as Mercs, but the general public tend to label all of us with this rather unflattering name. Being labelled as one of those low lifes annoys me because I'm not a Merc. I have standards; a code and I resent being tossed into the same pile as all the crazies who don't give a shit whether they bring in the right guy or the wrong guy or even kill them to bring them in. Mercs never engender affection from me and I would never do business with them. There have been times when I've found them tagging along behind me on a job and a couple of times they've tried to relieve me of my catch after sitting on my ass and watching me do all the work. Those types of occasions are the only ones where you're likely to see me really lose my rag. Knowing what I know now about this whole Nembier business, if I'd known any Mercs were shadowing me, I'd happily have offered them the job without a second thought.

As I said, I caught up with the liner in a few days and hailed them to let them know who I was and the reason for my visit. Cruise liners and the folks who run them are often a little unwilling to entertain folks like me because they're worried my presence will be bad for business but this one was one of those low budget outfits that don't take so much trouble to screen their passengers and crew as the more up market companies. This means that they know there's a higher than average chance that they could pick up a dodgy character as casual labour, and as they're more worried about themselves than their passengers, they tend to welcome me more openly in the hope I won't give them any problems with the Galactic Tourist Federation by reporting them.

"Unidentified ship, this is Captain Hann of the Nightliner Sally B. We are responding to your hail. Please identify yourself and state the nature of your business." The guy sounded calm so I guessed this was going to be a fairly trouble free encounter.

"Captain Hann, this is Sam Sinclair and this is my personal vessel, SC257. I'm here on official law enforcement business and wish to dock with you. Sending you my ID beacon and official tag now. Awaiting your response." A smile settled itself across my face as I sat back and waited for him to reply. There was no doubt in my mind that he would let me in without too much of a fuss; my official tag would ensure that but sometimes these types of people liked to try to psyche me out by keeping me waiting a little longer than necessary. That doesn't bother me too much; I'm happy to wait. As it happened, Captain Hann came back pretty quickly and I was a little surprised at the warmth of his welcome.

"Mr Sinclair we have your ID and tag. All seems to be in order. Come around to the rear dock, port six. Sending you the docking beacon now."

Captain Hann and his First Officer were there to meet me when I disembarked in the Sally B's rear dock. The place was shabby but functional, as would be expected on a low budget outfit like Nightline obviously was but Hann greeted me with a smile and a handshake, which is more than I often get on such occasions. They both nodded as I returned their smiles and shook their hands and they seemed happy when I accepted the Captain's offer of refreshment. Hann indicated for me to follow them to his office to discuss why I was there. As we walked I sneaked a look at him and smiled. He was in his early fifties I'd guess; probably ex military by the way he walked and his confident manner and his uniform was clean and sharp, despite the round gut that strained against his belt. He looked proud of his position and was obviously used to being in charge so I guessed he'd been an officer in his military days. As we left the functional areas of the liner behind and entered the public areas, the place became a whole lot cleaner. Here and there passengers passed us in the corridors and he greeted them all with a smile and a nod. This was a guy who wasn't used to trouble and didn't welcome the thought of it. He liked his easy life and his position, so anything able to threaten that was not going to be welcome here. This pleased me because it meant he was going to be only too happy to accommodate my requests so I could take the problem away for him. Over the years I've been doing this job I've met many people from all different planets and cultures and I've become something of an expert at reading people. Some of my colleagues in law enforcement quite rightly regard me as an excellent judge of character and Captain Hann wasn't about to prove me wrong.

His office was small and comfortable but still the military presence was everywhere; from the distinct lack of anything purely decorative to the precise arrangement of the few items on his desk. A digital log sat to his right, placed precisely between the communication panel and a single holographic photo viewer. To his left he placed his cap, after carefully wiping the badge that adorned the front with a pristine white handkerchief. Once he nudged the cap a few millimetres to the right, he sat down. My mind mentally drew up a list of what the holographic photo viewer displayed when switched on. At the top of the list was Hann himself as a younger man dressed in military uniform. Second was a group shot of him and some military buddies, whilst bringing up the rear was him receiving some award or promotion. The rank outsider was a dead heat between a landscape of some kind and a family group.

He offered me a seat and called for drinks to be brought in. "Well Mr Sinclair," he smiled, "what can we do for you?" He steepled his hands together as he looked at me from his side of the desk and the way his smile failed to reach the corners of his eyes told me right away that this was a bid for dominance.

Smiling back, I looked him right in the eyes. "I'm here to take one of your staff members into custody and deliver him into the hands of the appropriate authorities," I replied, my eyes still holding his.

His smile faltered and the steeple toppled. "Into custody? Who? and what for?"

My hand fumbled in my pocket for my data viewer and I tried not to smile at the way I'd expertly put him completely off his guard. He'd secretly hate me for it, but I didn't care. It was a victory; a small victory but a victory nonetheless and in this job you have to take the joy wherever you find it. As nonchalantly as I could, I tapped the screen and waited for a photograph of Nembier to pop up before handing it over.

"Professor Kluvak Nembier is his name," I said, "although you probably know him by some other name. He's wanted in connection with nine murders on Agrillia 3. I know he came aboard your vessel when you called into Agrillia a few days ago and I also know he wasn't on the passenger manifest so you must've hired him as casual labour." Hann and his second in command, to whom I still hadn't been introduced, studied the photo as I was speaking. Then something passed between them; a fleeting look that told me they knew who I was talking about.

"He's working as casual labour in stores," the second in command said as he glanced at me. "One of the staff had to leave suddenly due to a bereavement and we took this guy on to fill in. So far I haven't had any complaints from the other stores staff, so I assume he's doing the job okay."

"Nine murders you say?" Hann asked, his face now a little paler than when we first shook hands. His eyebrows shot to the top of his head as I nodded slowly and noticed the shock register in his expression. "Thank god he's not working with the passengers," he said quietly as he took a handkerchief from his pocket and mopped his brow. "Okay Mr Sinclair, what do you want us to do?"

Great. Now I had Hann's full co-operation the games could stop and I could get on with the job. "Thank you Captain," I smiled broadly, resisting the urge to steeple my own hands. That would just be rude and pompous I thought so I satisfied myself with a broad grin. "I presume you'd like this business to be conducted out of sight of your passengers?" He nodded furiously. "Do you have a plan of the liner so I can see the location of where he works?" The second in command, who I had already nicknamed Flark, tapped on a console and brought up a map of the area where Nembier worked.

"This is the stores here," he said as he pointed.

"And he works inside there? All the time?" I asked and he nodded. "Is there another way out?" Another nod and I swore. "Is he working right now?" Another nod. "What time does he get off?" Flark went to check and was back within a couple of minutes.

"Three hours till the end of his shift," he responded and I swore again. The last thing I wanted was for this to become an unseemly chase along corridors where paying passengers were likely to be wandering around. Then an idea suddenly presented itself to me and I smiled again.

"Does he have a room of his own or does he share?" I asked and breathed a sigh of relief when Flark told me he has his own quarters.

"Normally he'd be sharing with two other staff but as we have one in the infirmary and the other position still vacant, he's got the room to himself."

"Wonderful," I grinned. "Let's go."

Flark led the way down to the lower levels where the staff accommodation was situated and as we descended, the place became dirtier and shabbier. Hann used his Captain's password to over ride the private code on the entry system and we entered Nembier's room.

"Captain," I smiled. "Would you be so kind as to order Nembier back here to his room to help deal with a water leak in the bathroom?" Hann nodded and tapped the comms panel on the wall by the door. Nembier's bathroom was no bigger than the wash cubicle on board my ship and offered just a basin, toilet and single shower cubicle. The basin to my left offered just enough space for someone to wash their hands and I was pleased to notice it was even smaller than mine as I turned both taps on full blast, before indicating to Hann and Flark to hide behind the door. We pressed ourselves against the wall and waited.

Five minutes later we heard the click as the security system accepted Nembier's pass code and unlocked the door. Gun in hand, I held my breath as the door opened and a small wiry man entered. Before he took his third step across the room the sedative dart hit him square in the nape of the neck. Within twenty seconds he was on the floor and out for the count and I was securing his hands and feet. After hauling him up onto the bed I turned and smiled at Hann and Flark.

"Thank you for you co-operation Captain. Job done quick and clean. Wish they were all as easy as this one," I said as I returned to the bathroom and turned off the taps.

"No problem Mr Sinclair," Hann nodded as he ran a hand through his hair and straightened his shirt. "Is there anything else we can do to help?"

This guy was being so nice it was almost embarrassing. Forcing myself not to laugh, I nodded. "Yes actually there is. Do you have somewhere secure I could use to interview him? The rules dictate that I go through the proper procedure before taking him back to the authorities. Y'know a formal interview so that he knows why he's being held and what his rights are?"

He nodded and turned to Flark. "Can you arrange for one of the quarantine units in the infirmary to be made available as soon as possible?" Flark nodded and left the room and Hann nodded to me. "The infirmary has three quarantine units just in case of a breakout of something virulently contagious infecting the ship. They are completely secure and private and you're welcome to use one of them for as long as you need."

This was very helpful. Quite often I end up doing these interviews in bathrooms, cupboards and all manner of places, so to have the use of a proper facility would make things much more comfortable and reminded me of my days as a desk bound official in Law Enforcement. In those days I had more responsibility and all the back up I could ask for, without too much of the dirty work. Good hours, good facilities and good pay. Trouble was I was bored to fuck with the predictability and safeness of it all. The petty rules and regulations I was forced to stick to irritated me no end and so many times I had to sit back and let some asshole walk out the door because of some rule or stupid regulation. In the end I knew something had to give and it was either give it up or go freelance. Over the years I'd built up a decent network of contacts and I was good at my job; I enjoyed it and wasn't about to just throw it all away so I handed in my uniform and office keys, took possession of an ex law enforcement official tag, used up a sizeable portion of my savings to buy my own ship and went freelance. The thrill of the chase took years off me and the freedom to do what I do well without the constriction of petty regulations was like a burden lifted off my shoulders for the first time. My very first job after going freelance was the happiest time I'd known in years and I swear I had a grin on my face the whole damn time. It was still nice to be offered decent facilities in which to do my job though and I smiled at Hann.

"Thanks Captain, that'll do nicely. When he wakes up I'll get him installed in there and hopefully we should both be out of your hair within a few hours and on our way to Floxham Island."

His eyebrows shot up in surprise. "Floxham Island? You're taking him there?"

"Yeah."

"Well there's no need to rush off then. We're stopping there so why not stay on board and enjoy a few days relaxation?" This news surprised me and I must have looked bemused because Hann sniggered at my expression. It's one of my regular delivery points as it's in a main shipping lane and easy for the authorities to get to for trials and sentencing hearings. Why would a passenger liner be calling there? Even a low budget outfit like Nightliner surely had no need to call into that place.

"Why the hell are you calling there?"

"It's one of our regular stops Mr Sinclair. As you are no doubt aware, Nightliner isn't exactly the most elite cruise line in the business." He was right, I was very aware of this fact from the moment I came aboard. "We deliver a supply of a few luxuries whenever we pass by the Floxham system that the staff isn't afforded by the Law Enforcement Agency and we usually have a few people wishing to visit with family members who work or are incarcerated there. We drop the supplies and the visitors, along with a shuttle lander and crew and leave them there whilst we continue on to The Oasis for a day of sun and relaxation. We then return to pick up the visitors and carry on our way. You're more than welcome to remain on board with us until we reach Floxham and if you don't fancy spending three days down there in their visitor's accommodations, you can use your own vessel once we get there. It'll give you a few days to relax and save you some fuel and of course, the Sally B's facilities are at your disposal free of charge."

You can call me all sorts of names, and even the unpleasant ones will sometimes be deserved but stupid will never be one of them. A few days relaxing on a cruise liner free of charge while my prisoner was safely stowed away. Was I interested?

"Well that's extremely kind of you Captain," I smiled and nodded. "I'd be happy to accept your hospitality." He nodded back and seemed relieved that I'd accepted his offer. It was obvious to me that he took this as a sign that I was unlikely to report him to the authorities for taking Nembier on without the proper checks and he was right. At the end of the day all I'm interested in is getting to my target. People break rules all the time; hell I break rules all the time and it wouldn't serve me to take the time and effort to report Hann for taking on some casual labour. Besides, building a good working relationship with him might come in handy at some time in the future and I'm always aware of the benefits of having a good network of contacts. It's what my job is built on and without them, I'd be out of a job. Like I said before, I'm not stupid and I'm also well aware of the potential benefits that come from letting him think I might just decide to report him!

Hann suggested he call for a medical team to transport Nembier to the quarantine bay on a stretcher so that if any passengers saw him, they'd assume he was sick and being taken to the infirmary. He didn't want his passengers getting upset by seeing a guy in restraints. That's understandable so I agreed and we were soon escorting a still unconscious Nembier to the quarantine bay where he was installed to wake up. After I removed his restraints and the room was secured, a doctor examined him and estimated he'd be out for a couple of hours so Hann suggested he find me a room where I could take a shower and change my clothes before having a meal with him. The Sally B is a big liner with a large number of rooms but I was expecting to be installed within a cubicle no bigger than the firearms locker on board my ship, seeing as I was not paying for the pleasure but to my complete surprise I found myself being given a large room with private bathroom.

"Very nice room Captain, thank you very much," I said and meant every word.

"You're very welcome Mr Sinclair. You have done us a favour by getting rid of a murderer who could potentially have caused havoc on board and we are very grateful." He'd got one up on me and he knew it; my surprise at the luxury of the room he'd given me gave him the upper hand. That didn't bother me really; I'd got my man and now had a few days in which to relax at no expense to myself so I was happy to give a bit of ground in our little power game. "Dinner is in an hour. The dining hall is on deck three. Just give your name to the man on the door and he'll show you to my table. There's no dress code by the way." Now he was kicking me in the groin. Not only had he gained a point by giving me this nice room but that remark was just gratuitous point scoring and I was annoyed.

"Okay Captain I'll look forward to it and thank you again for your hospitality." He was still smiling to himself as he let himself out and I supposed he was laughing quietly to himself all the way back to his office. A quick trip back to my ship to collect what belongings I felt I might need was my next course of action and within twenty minutes I was enjoying a wonderful hot shower. Although I live and work in my ship for months at a time, I have a shower on board; don't get me wrong I have all the facilities I need but they're basic. This however, was luxury after what I'm used to and gave me an opportunity to take a bit of care over my appearance for a change.

The job I do doesn't often call for me to look like I've just stepped out of a clothes store and I'm no male model but I do okay for myself. You couldn't honestly call me the worst looking guy in the galaxy and when I do get the opportunity to take some care, I can turn a head or two. My home world is Sigma Prime and we're lucky because we're known as a good looking race. Sigma men tend to be solidly built and firm and others tend to describe us as having enigmatic good looks, whatever that means. Once I was showered I looked out the best shirt I had and a fresh pair of pants and took a long, hard look in the mirror. The need for a haircut was obvious to me right away and I made a vow to seek out a hairdresser right after dinner. There's no way I'm the vainest guy around but I do like my hair to be good and as I looked at my reflection I was not totally happy. My job keeps me in shape okay but I realised that from the neck up, I looked tired. Not only was my hair a bit neglected but my face looked a little stressed. Okay so I had a plan; dinner, interview Nembier then a haircut and a dermal.

Nembier was still a little bleary eyed when I went to do the interview with him but at least he was awake enough for me to do what I had to do so I could get to my appointment with the hairdresser and skin therapist. As an official law enforcement freelancer, there is a set procedure I have to go through once I've captured my target. It's not my job to ascertain anyone's guilt or innocence but I do have to make sure I have the right guy and let them know why they're being restrained and what I intend to do with them. Digging out my digital scanner, I brought up Nembier's fingerprint record, retinal scan and DNA record and entered the quarantine room.

"Good afternoon Professor Nembier," I smiled.

"Huh?" he grunted as he ran a hand through his hair and avoided my eyes. "What the fuck are you talking about? My name is Tallion." It was hard for me to suppress a snigger as I prepared a fresh blood sampler.

"Well okay let's find out shall we?" I challenged as I turned to face him, blood sampler and scanner in hand. "Hold out your thumb please, this won't hurt a bit." My eyes locked challengingly into his as I took a second step towards him and he backed away. "What's up Mr umm Tallion," I said as I took a third step forward. "It won't hurt; I just need a blood sample to prove you are indeed Mr Tallion and not Professor Nembier as I first thought." He backed away a bit more, his eyes never leaving the blood sampler in my hand.

"I umm, I don't like the sight of blood," he offered. This statement almost made me whoop out loud with glee and I mentally gave myself a high five as he unwittingly helped me win the bet I'd placed with myself. In this job you have to find your entertainment wherever you can and as I said, I like to think of myself as an excellent judge of character. It has become a habit for me to continually test my people skills and one of the things I do is try to guess which excuse the target will use first to avoid the blood sampler. The two most often used are a fear of needles and not liking the sight of blood. Nembier struck me right away as a guy who was okay with needles. He's not the type to fret over something silly like a blood sampler so I went with him hating the sight of blood and he'd just won me another fifty. It took all my control not to thank him.

"Don't worry Mr Tallion you won't see any blood," I assured him in my most authoritative tone as I took a fourth step towards him. "This unit is completely self contained and everything is done inside the thumb sleeve." That fourth step took me too far inside his comfort zone and he leapt up and backed across the room yelling at me to get away. Sighing with annoyance, I turned and nodded to the medical aides who I had already arranged to be watching through the one way glass and waited for them to enter and restrain him. Two mountainous men entered and approached him assertively and had him firmly restrained within seconds. Within another thirty seconds I got my blood sample, took a scan of his fingerprint and retina and within another two minutes I confirmed him as being Professor Kluvak Nembier. He sat on the edge of the bed as I packed away my scanner and blood sampler and I watched him closely as I clicked on my digital recorder. A weird feeling coursed through me and I suddenly felt sorry for the guy as he sat there with his head in his hands looking scared and for a moment I could've almost believed him to be innocent.

"Professor Kluvak Nembier," I said as I began the speech that was so familiar. "My name is Sinclair. I am a Freelance Law Enforcer, tag reference code Sinclair 27593-4/167AZP and it is my duty to inform you that I now place you under restraint as per warrant code AZ267/M. You shall remain under restraint until such time as I deliver you into the care of the relevant authorities on

Floxham 4 where you are to be questioned in connection with nine murders on Agrillia 3." After noting the date and time, I clicked off the recorder and scanned it into the record along with the identification details I'd taken from him. "Thank you very much for your co-operation Professor," I smiled as I turned and left the room. If I hurried I might still make that haircut appointment.

She seemed delighted when I gave her a large tip. She'd done an excellent job on my hair and I was genuinely pleased as I checked myself out in the mirror in her salon on deck five. Not too much off, just a tidy up and a zap of Tricholox to thicken it up and give it more body. Tricholox is marvellous stuff for those of us not blessed with naturally thick and luxuriant hair. I'm no scientist so the minutiae of how it works isn't exactly my thing. All I know is that after they give you several injections all over your scalp it makes the hair twice as thick as it is naturally and lasts for three or four months before needing a top up. She smiled and I winked at her as I left the salon and headed next door for my dermal appointment. A pretty red headed gal smiled at me as I entered and gave my name. She offered me a drink while I waited and I was soon enjoying a cold Andolian beer. A leggy blonde appeared and bade me follow her into a cubicle where I was soon hooked up to a dermal optimiser. This machine is a one step skin perfecting machine that cleans, smoothes, tightens and freshens all in one go. Cold goo is spread all over the face and then they put this thin fabric mask thing over the top. The machine has a sort of helmet that comes down over your face like a close fitting space helmet and when they switch it on you can feel your skin tingle and the muscles of the face tighten up. It feels strange but it's not painful and when you're done, the whole effect is a cleaner, fresher and younger looking face. When the procedure was finished I was pleased. In the space of one afternoon I'd got my man restrained, been installed within a first class cabin with private bathroom and offered a free cruise, had my hair seen to and several years taken off my face. The leggy blonde also received a large tip along with my Unicom number just in case, and I went to check out what other delights the liner offered.

CHAPTER TWO

As I think back now, I've been doing this job for almost fifteen years and in all that time I haven't taken much time off and I can't remember the last time I actually had a holiday, so when Captain Hann offered me the run of the liner for the three days it would take to get to Floxham 4, I took full advantage. Apart from checking in with Nembier every day to make sure he was behaving himself, my time was my own and I spent my days relaxing by the pool on the sun deck and my nights enjoying the leggy blonde. Boy did she know how to please a guy and it was with more than a little reluctance that I checked in with Hann on the morning before our arrival at Floxham 4 to thank him for his hospitality.

"Thank you Captain for your hospitality," I smiled as I extended my hand. "I'll have Nembier installed in my ship once we get into orbit around Floxham and we'll be out of your hair." He shook my hand and offered me a seat before making me an offer I still don't know to this day I was wise to accept. It seemed like the sensible thing to do at the time so I didn't hesitate and maybe the leggy blonde was partly to blame.

"You're very welcome Mr Sinclair but there's really no need to take your own ship down to Floxham. As I told you when you first arrived on board, we have supplies and visitors to deliver to the prison, after which the liner continues on to The Oasis. After a day in the sun we return to pick up the visitors, before continuing with the cruise. If you wish, you can tag along in our shuttle for the trip and continue with us after we return to pick you all up; at least until you get yourself another job. You're more than welcome to remain on board for as long as you wish and I will admit that having an official law enforcer on board is good for passenger morale."

This was the defining moment of the job. Looking back on it now in the cold light of day, I could've done so many things differently but at the time it seemed the obvious thing to do and despite everything, I was beginning to like Hann and our little power game that I was happy to let him win so he would remain gracious and helpful. It didn't take me long to accept and the thought of spending a few more nights with the blonde's long legs wrapped round me was more than a little persuasive. Memories of her and the skill with which she lured me into a state of complete euphoria soon had me smiling as I returned to my room to packed my stuff before making a trip to my ship for anything I thought I might need, and how many times since then I've wondered whether I made the right decision, I can't begin to count.

An area at the rear of the shuttle was blocked off with some spare wall boards so Nembier could be adequately restrained without the passengers getting upset at seeing him. Two of Hann's security guards returned with me to the quarantine room and together with the two mountainous medical aides who helped me get the blood sample from him three days before, the five of us had him installed within the shuttle without a fuss. Hann shook my hand once again as the passengers and crew loaded and I was pleased to see that Flark, who I found out was actually called Commander Morry Laymon, would be Captain for our sojourn to Floxham. Try as I might, I just couldn't see him as Morry; he'd always be Flark to me. Thirty minutes later we left the belly of the Sally B and headed down towards Floxham Island. It would make me feel a whole lot better about things if I was able to say that I had some inner dread as we approached the prison but I'd be unnecessarily dramatic and totally wrong if I did. It was with relative calm that I whistled to myself and looked at the other passengers and not once did I feel any kind of dark cloud inside, no deep foretelling of impending doom hammering at my skull to put me on my guard. Since then I've wished so often that I did have some kind of dark foreboding that day; many lives would've been saved if I had but then many more might've been doomed to be lost later on.

Let me tell you a little about Floxham Island, just so you can get the feel of the place. It's one of my regular delivery points so I've been there a few times with what I call my cargo and it's not a place I really enjoy visiting. Floxham 4 is an uninhabited planet with a mountainous and deeply forested environment. Although I say uninhabited that's not strictly true; it is inhabited but not by people. A long time ago the Inter Galactic Law Enforcement Agency decided, in its wisdom, to build an outpost there where prisoners could be tried, sentenced and incarcerated all in the one place and where all of the forensic testing and evidence could be processed on site. They cleared several square miles of forest but before they could begin to build, they had to dig a deep trench three hundred feet deep and five hundred across. The purpose of the trench was to keep the indigenous animal life out of the complex so the builders could do their job in safety. You see, Floxham 4 is home to huge predatory creatures; millions of them roam the entire planet and no one would survive long beyond that trench. That's one of the main reasons they built the prison there; the knowledge of the creatures ensures none of the prisoners dare try to escape.

The prison is a self contained living environment, like a small town and not only houses the prisoners and the staff but also has accommodations for visitors and those who work in the other aspects of law enforcement; judges and court officials etc. Those who visit family members incarcerated there are allowed a three day visit twice a year and they spend the whole three days down there and the accommodations are comfortable despite it being a prison. The food is good and the staff know how to have a good time and I didn't mind being stuck there for three days with Nembier. It's my job not just to deliver my cargo, but also to go through some official stuff with regard to the case, do my report and officially hand them over and that normally takes the better part of a day anyway. The leggy blonde wouldn't be there, which was a shame but there's always the hope of a sexy female judge to help me while away the time.

The prison's automated comms system welcomed us as soon as we arrived at the planet, and guided us down to the landing station that we could see framed in dull glowing yellow lights below us. Sneaking a look at my fellow passengers as we descended, I tried to get a handle on them. People watching is fun and I suppose it's because of my job that I've become so good at reading people and I find myself automatically summing people up whenever I meet them, even when there's no need. It's a habit I've got into and I don't feel the need to stop doing it just yet. They were a mixed bunch; one old man with a young kid by his side, two guys who looked to be in their twenties, one of whom had dark brown skin and bright eyes, a teenage girl and a nice but rather plain young woman. One of the guys, the solidly built man with deep brown skin was obviously military; the way he held himself and his firm gaze told me that right away. The other guy looked a bit soft and seemed to be more of a thinker than a doer. The plain woman looked tough and I knew instantly that here was one tough gal that didn't need a man by her side to make her feel complete. This woman looked the type who would argue with you and know she could hold her own in any debate. She was one of those women who believe that she has what it takes to survive in any situation, but lacks any actual experience of having to do so. The teenage girl looked scared and frail but I could tell she had an amazing strength inside of her that she hadn't needed to discover yet. It was the old guy and the kid who really caught my attention though and I knew right away that there was a lot that old guy was hiding. He made me feel uneasy but I didn't know why and the kid didn't make me feel any better. As I looked into the kid's eyes it was as if he didn't quite belong in that body somehow. He made me shiver inwardly and I looked away.

We had five crew on board with us; Flark was Captain and under him was a pilot by the name of Chip Trale; a blonde, blue eyed plank who obviously felt he should've been a model or a vidicom star instead. His co pilot was at the opposite end of the scale and the contrast between them was more than a little amusing. Luggs was a throwback to some time long ago when his race was first evolving from grunting animals. A coarse individual, he was big but lacked grace when he moved and seemed to have a permanent and unsettling leer on his face. If I was a woman I'd feel very uncomfortable around him. The navigator was our one female crew member and I felt let down as I looked at her. Meesha Roddry was obviously a gal who liked a drink and probably used it to mask out some past hurt that she hadn't yet come to terms with. She looked at every male on board in a way that made it very clear she'd open her legs for anyone without a fuss, even the old guy. We also had an engineer with us by the name of Jo Cappilianos who told everyone to call him Cap. He was one of those annoyingly happy folks with a permanent smile on his face who never worries about anything and is always optimistic and joyful. The kind of guy you like to punch first thing on a Sunday morning after a heavy evening the night before.

We landed safely on Floxham Island's shuttle landing station and everyone prepared to disembark. Hann and I had previously arranged for the passengers to disembark first, while I would wait inside with the crew before escorting Nembier into the prison. Once the passengers were off, I got up and began to take down the wall boards shielding him from view. I was just about to say something to Flark when the scream rang out and everyone was shocked into silence. Everyone looked at each other before jumping up and heading for the hatch to see what the commotion was. As we followed the direction of the scream we could hear sobbing. It was late afternoon and the light was getting low when we arrived and the dull yellow landing lights didn't afford us much illumination so it wasn't until we were within a few feet that we could see the teenage girl sobbing and being comforted by the plain woman.

"What's going on here?" Flark bellowed. The woman pointed into the gloom to her left and we all squinted but could see nothing. Luggs took a step closer and we heard him gasp in shock before swearing and turning away to vomit. "What the fuck is going on Luggs?" Flark bellowed again and Luggs pointed. He and Cap approached cautiously and peered into the darkness. "Holy fuck," Flark exclaimed as he jumped back. By now I was getting more curious myself so I took a step forward but he blocked my way. "I wouldn't if I were you Mr Sinclair," he gasped as he looked at me wide eyed. There was no way I was missing out on the fun so I stepped past him and took a look and found myself staring into a pair of startled eyes. The hat told me this was one of the prison guards and his shocked expression was obviously a result of him having no body below the chest; the gaping, bloody rent through which we could clearly see ribs, lungs and liver telling us this guy met with a horrible end not long ago. The shock made me leap back and I glared at Flark.

"What the fuck?" I began but couldn't think how to finish. Before anyone could say anything else we heard a loud roaring grunt and everyone looked around. Having been here before, I knew there were terrible creatures living on Floxham but I'd never heard them so

close before and it unsettled me. The noise came again and Flark
sprang into action, bellowing commands and ordering everyone to
run for the main door of the prison. Shaking away my shock, I leapt
back into the shuttle to unlock Nembier and Luggs appeared beside
me; his size helping to ensure that my prisoner would give us no
trouble. Nembier looked scared, his eyes darting to and fro and he
obviously picked up on our unease. Feeling no desire to allay his
fears I grabbed my bag and dragged him from the shuttle; Luggs
holding his other arm in a vice like grip.

We leapt from the hatch and raced to catch up with the others
who were by now over a hundred yards ahead of us. We heard
another loud roar right behind us and I turned to find myself looking
at something I'd never seen before and never want to see again. That
image haunted my dreams for weeks afterwards and almost drove me
to drink. The creature was two legged but hunched forward; the
hump on its back giving it a slightly bent forward appearance. It
didn't appear to have arms that I could see, but its head was huge and
out of all proportion to the size of its body and I couldn't help
wondering how the hell it supported such a huge head. The head was
basically spherical, if rather flat on top, with a wedge shaped jaw
jutting from the front with rather short but wickedly pointed teeth in
two rows, top and bottom. The thing that surprised me most was its
eyes and as I looked at them I realised two things that save our lives.
First I realised that we had no hope of out running this thing; with
two hundred yards of open space between us and the safety of the
prison, we were screwed. As I continued looking at that horrific face
I realised why those eyes surprised me; they were tiny and the way it
was moving its head told me those eyes were almost useless.
Realising that this meant it probably worked off sound or smell or
both, I scanned the head again for ears and noticed a large hole on
each side, surrounded by what looked like a bony frill. It obviously
uses sound far more than sight so I put on my most commanding
whisper.

"Keep still guys," I hissed as loudly as I dared. "Don't move a
muscle and keep silent."

"What the fuck?" Luggs started to protest but I shushed him
immediately.

"Shut the fuck up you idiot, it can't see. Look at its eyes, they're useless. It operates on sound so shut the fuck up and keep still okay?" Surprisingly, Luggs did as he was told and we stood there; the three of us rooted to the spot as the huge creature approached, turning its head this way and that, scanning for sounds. At one point that huge head passed by my face with just a couple of inches to spare and I felt and smelled its acrid breath. Nembier was terrified out of his wits; I could feel him shaking as I held onto him and I'd already decided that if he ran off screaming like a kid, I wasn't going to chase after him this time. It was then that I was suddenly reminded of some of those old vidicom movies I love so much as we stood there within twenty feet of the creature as it slowly approached, head bobbing from side to side, ears cocked for the slightest noise. After what seemed like an hour but was probably less than a couple of minutes, the creature snorted and lumbered away to the right and disappeared into the gloom. We waited until we could no longer hear its footsteps thudding before running for our lives towards the prison. We caught up with the rest of the group as they reached the main door. We stopped to get our breath and make sure everyone was accounted for and found that so far at least, we hadn't lost anyone.

"Oh fuck. Fuck what the hell was that?" Luggs said, his voice trembling with fear. "My god, what the fuck was that?" The guy was obviously terrified but I had to hand it to him, he held onto his fear and I felt some admiration for him.

"This whole planet is full of them," I said and he nodded.

"I know that but why the fuck is it here on the island?" he asked, knowing I hadn't a clue.

"Fuck knows," I said as I shrugged my shoulders. "The trench is supposed to keep them all out. Come on let's get inside where it's safe huh?" He nodded and with a last fearful look behind, we entered the prison.

Once we got inside and shut the door we all thought we would be safe. We expected the prison staff to come running up and ask us if we were okay or had we lost anyone and would we like a drink to settle our nerves but the place was eerily silent. The teenage girl was still crying and being comforted by the plain woman who was in her element having someone to take charge of. At that moment I realised that although rather a plain looking woman, she would be very useful in a crisis and I silently apologised to her for underestimating her worth. My mind was still trying to digest what just happened to us out there and I suppose a part of me still didn't quite believe it. Usually I'm not given to fits of panic but at that moment a part of me was silently screaming for help.

"Is everyone here? Do we have everyone?" Flark barked suddenly, breaking the silence of the place and making us jump as his voice echoed around the room. We all looked at each other and realised that yeah, we'd all made it. "Is anyone hurt? Are there any injuries?" he barked again.

"Does shitting my pants count?" Luggs retorted immediately and a tense silence ensued before one by one, we all started to laugh. Even Nembier was grinning at that. It's funny how, during high stress situations, things make you laugh that might not in another situation. It's like it's a survival mechanism for stress relief or something. Normally I would have found Luggs disgusting but that made me laugh and I realised that here was another good ally to have in a crisis, despite him being a little coarse. Although I didn't yet realise it, subconsciously I was picking my team for when the shit really hit the fan, which was in just a few minutes.

"Why is he in restraints?" the military guy asked suddenly and everyone now looked at Nembier, who blushed to the roots of his hair and looked at the floor. In the panic I'd forgotten that no one knew about him and for a moment I tried to think of a plausible lie, before realising I'd just have to tell them the truth.

"He's my prisoner," I replied, "and I brought him here for trial."

"What did he do?" military guy enquired.

"Nothing, I'm innocent," Nembier suddenly interrupted.

"Aren't they all?" I snorted in reply as I looked around for somewhere to secure him. A corridor stretched out ahead so I opened a couple of doors and found one to be a bathroom. It wasn't the ideal place to house a prisoner but circumstances dictated that I think on my feet, so I dragged him inside and cuffed him around a metal girder that held the mezzanine ceiling up. He protested of course and I promised to come back and move him once we'd gotten our bearings and found some guards who could take charge of him. He gave me no trouble but as I turned to leave he called me back.

"Sinclair?" he called and I turned and looked at him. "Don't leave me alone in here too long huh? Whatever you think of me is irrelevant; just don't forget me, please." That was another of those moments when I really wondered about Nembier so I nodded and left the room.

Pretty soon we realised that our arrival should have been noticed by now and the lack of any staff coming to check us out became too obvious to ignore. It was then that I had a thought that scared me so much I instinctively backed away from it. There was no way I wanted that thought; I didn't want it at all but it wouldn't go away no matter what I tried. My mind forced me to consider the possibility that the staff hadn't come to see us because they were all dead. The fact that no one else voiced the question made me realise that they were probably trying not to acknowledge the same thought themselves. Finally I knew someone had to take the lead if we wanted to get out of this alive so I voiced what no one else wanted to.

"Why is there no staff here? Shouldn't someone have come to check us out already? Is everyone here dead from those creatures?" Blank faces looked back at me as I looked from one person to the next so I turned to Flark; instinct telling me to give the problem to the Captain. "Well?" I demanded as I raised my eyebrows. "Where the fuck is everyone?"

"How the fuck should I know?" he countered angrily and glared at me. His response surprised me; I was taken aback by his aggressive tone and was about to respond in kind when it occurred to me that he was obviously scared shitless. He sighed deeply and I remembered that he was employed by a cruise line and more than likely has never been in anything remotely similar to this situation before. This made me feel bad, a little, so I backed off. The last thing this situation needed was a row when we needed to work together.

"Sorry Captain," I replied and nodded at him. "Maybe we should take a look around huh? Maybe split into a couple of groups and meet up back here in an hour, what do you think? Is everyone okay with that?" Hoping everyone would agree I looked around the group and everyone nodded and grunted in response. It was the only sensible thing to do anyway. Working alone all the time means I don't have to answer to anyone and I was about to suggest who goes with whom when I remembered that Flark was technically in charge of us so I held my tongue. "Captain? You wanna suggest who goes with whom?" I offered.

He looked at me and nodded. "Okay folks, we have 2 kids with us so maybe we should first find a secure room and hide them in there while the rest of us split up to search the place okay?" Everyone began to nod but the old guy with the weird kid looked aghast and clasped the boy's hand tighter as he shook his head violently.

"No, I'm sorry Captain but I can't leave Eddy alone," the old guy said. "He stays with me or I stay with him." My heart sank and I gave a silent sigh and rolled my eyes as I remembered all those vidicom movies where this happens and the kid ends up running off and getting everyone killed. Flark was obviously thinking the same thing because his expression darkened and I mentally clapped him on the back.

"Listen to me dammit," he snapped. "You saw what was out there and for all we know this whole place could be crawling with them and who knows what else. We have to take a look around to see what we're dealing with and we don't want to have to deal with 2 scared kids when we might have to fight for our lives. Now we find a secure room and Eddy and the girl can keep each other company there while the rest of us reccy the place. That's an order not a suggestion by the way so get with it people." His expression made it clear it would be unwise to argue so we moved off and within a couple of minutes we found a small office with a lockable door. We arranged the desks and chairs to make a little den and put Eddy and the girl down in there together. The girl looked scared to be left on her own and I felt sorry for her. She'd been no trouble at all so far and was travelling alone and must've been scared out of her wits. Her eyes were huge and frightened as I crouched down and smiled at her and gave her hand a squeeze.

"Hi there, my name's Sam," I smiled. "What's yours?"

"Jena Marks," she replied quietly.

"That's a pretty name," I continued. "Now Jena, you're a real grown up young lady so I want you to do an important job for me okay? Do you think you can do that?" She nodded and stopped crying. "Great. Now Eddy here is real scared so he needs you to be brave for him." She nodded. "You're the only one I can trust with him." She nodded again. "Good girl. Now we will be back in an hour, after we've had a look around so don't think we've forgotten you. We'll come back for you in one hour, I promise."

"Can you find my dad and bring him back?" she asked quietly and I frowned.

"Your Dad?" I asked and then realised he must be an inmate. "Oh is he an inmate here? What's his name?"

"No he works here," she replied. "His name is Randy Marks and he's a guard. We're going on holiday together to Arrenar Prime."

"Oh I see," I nodded and smiled. "I'll look out for him okay?" This seemed to placate her a little so I smiled and stood up. It was only then that I saw what the old guy was doing. He was crouched down beside Eddy and was gesturing to him with his hands. At no time did he speak, but continued gesturing until the boy nodded and scooted over next to Jena. As I turned to leave the room I caught sight of the thinker guy and his expression made me stop in my tracks. He was watching the old guy with a frown, which soon turned to shock. Before I could ask him what was up, Flark barked at us once more.

"Okay people listen up. There are ten of us so we'll split up into two groups of three and one of four and scout the place out and be back here in one hour. I've found a plan of the complex. Here look." He spread out the large sheet on one of the desks. The prison was laid out in the typical way, with a large oblong central building with eight long wings leading off it in a semi circle like the rays of a sun. "This central section is where we are now and there are four floors, so I vote for now we contain our search to this central building first. Now who here is competent with firearms?" The military guy, the plain woman, Meesha, Cap, Luggs and me all raised our hands. "Okay," Flark continued. "This room here," he said pointing to a small square on the plan, "is the armoury so I vote we make our way there first before we split up. We must make sure each group has at least one competent gun with them too. Any questions? Okay let's go."

Slowly we made our way to the armoury and let ourselves in. This was somewhere I immediately felt at home so I knew what I was looking for. It didn't take long for me to find the appropriate hardware and I helped myself to a powerful short range laser rifle and a laser pistol. As I helped myself to several spare ammo clips, I saw the thinker guy looking bemused so I went over and introduced myself.

"Sam Sinclair," I said, extending my hand, which he shook nervously.

"Ronjo Beghart," he replied.

"Ever fired a gun?"

"Never, but I sure wish I had," he smiled. He was obviously scared so I took pity on him and took a quick look around to see what was most appropriate from the hardware on display and smiled when my eyes fell upon a rack of rookies. The AB11 Rookie is the first weapon given to new military recruits, many of whom will never have used a firearm before. The Rookie has a very short effective range but it's lightweight and easy to load and fire. Reaching up, I fetched a couple down with several spare ammo clips.

"Here ya go," I smiled. "Anyone with a few brain cells can use one of these; they're real easy. Just hold it like this, aim and fire. Each of these clips here will give you a hundred shots and when you're empty you just pull this here, like this. Drop it and click another one in like this. Here, you try." Crossing my fingers that he was a swift learner, I watched as he changed the clip remarkably well and smiled at me. It's always been a firm belief of mine that an armed man will feel safer in even the most hopeless of circumstances and I reckoned there was always a chance that this guy might just save my hide before we got off this rock. Once we were all armed we split up and I found myself teamed up with Luggs, Cap and Ronjo. Not a bad haul considering what else was on offer. We decided to take the second floor so with a deep breath, we set off up the stairs.

CHAPTER THREE

My mood was almost fearless as we began climbing the stairs but as we continued climbing and the silence closed in around us, a sense of unease again crept in. As we reached the second floor I'd decided that I was mighty glad to have Luggs nearby and mentally apologised to him for my low opinion earlier. A throwback to ancient times he may be, but he was damn fearless and ready to take anything on. He strode forward with purpose and I couldn't help but admire him. Embarrassed at not being the first to move, I tried to emulate him and strode after him. Cap was behind me and Ronjo, shaking with fear, crept along at the back. Looking back on what we must've looked like as we crept our way around the second floor offices; a fearless throwback, a law enforcer, a terminally optimistic engineer and a terrified civilian, I can't help but laugh and although we were a motley bunch, we were no pushover.

The first three offices we found revealed nothing of any use to us, either by way of explanation or assistance and we were beginning to relax as we continued down the corridor. Luggs snorted with annoyance and swore as he hefted the ridiculously large laser rifle he'd helped himself to in the armoury. It turned out that he was ex military too and was firearms trained so we felt safer with another competent gun in our group. As he continued onwards with his huge gun at the ready, he reminded me of one of those characters in vidicom games. You know the type; massive shoulders and eyebrow ridges to match and no language to speak of other than the occasional grunt. Oh and always the obligatory huge gun. Even his name matched the look and I couldn't help but smile.

We approached the fourth office in the corridor and saw at once that something awful had happened here. The remains of the door lay in pieces on the floor and the bit that remained hung flaccidly on its remaining hinge; giving silent testament to some previous and terrible assault. Each of the pieces bore huge scratches almost an inch deep and as I looked, I couldn't imagine what manner of beast made them, nor with what. We looked at each other, eyebrows raised and eyes wide in shock as we took in the scene.

"What the hell could've made those scratches?" Ronjo exclaimed, verbalising the thought each of us was silently wrestling with.

"More to the point," Luggs said, "is it still inside there?"

"Well you're more than welcome to go and find out," Ronjo responded immediately, "and I'll wait out here for ya."

"On your own?" Luggs grinned at him. "Sure buddy, okay. See ya later," he snorted as he stepped towards the door and ducked under the wood that hung limp from the wrenched hinge. There was no way I was about to drop any further down the pecking order just yet, so I stepped in after him, swiftly followed by Cap. The interior of the room looked like the aftermath of a hurricane. One desk was smashed to matchwood; the other was still in one piece but upside down with one leg bent at a most unnatural angle. The remains of computer consoles lay in pieces on the floor amongst other assorted debris; the flotsam and jetsam of prison administration cast unceremoniously aside in what must've been one hell of an attack. Cap produced a flashlight and swung it around the room and we all saw the body at once. Propped up in one corner, the abdomen flared open to display the contents within that none of us wanted to see.

"Holy fuck," Luggs exclaimed as we heard Ronjo gasp behind us and run out into the corridor; his heaving and gagging almost as unsettling as the sight that lay before us.

The man sat in the corner, his eyes staring unseeing into the room. One arm hung down, hand in his lap while the other was tucked behind his back. The two flaps of skin splayed apart as the contents tumbled out into his crotch, reminding me of those darkly gothic and cheaply made vidicom horror movies I watch from time to time. Cap trained his flashlight on it and the bloody mass glistened at us as we stood there revolted but unable to look away.

"Whatever the fuck killed him ate his insides but didn't touch anything else," Cap whispered. Unsure of what he was getting at, I frowned and he nodded to the body. "Look at the rest of him Sam, not a scratch on him." We looked and found to our horror that he was right; whatever killed the man was only interested in what lay beneath the skin. Luggs and I came to the same realisation at the same instant as Cap said what we were thinking. "That means he was alive when it started eating him."

We found Ronjo breathing deeply out in the corridor and set off once again. Up ahead the corridor turned ninety degrees to the left and no matter how hard I tried, I couldn't help but imagine all sorts of horrors waiting for us around that corner. It occurred to me that the others might be thinking the same and I almost asked them in an effort to lighten the mood, but then realised that Ronjo would probably lose it if I did, so I held my tongue. What we found were three more bodies, all with their insides torn out but otherwise untouched and the floor was sticky underfoot with congealed blood. We squelched past them and headed for the nearest office to find it ransacked in a similar manner to the last one. The corridor walls were littered with the same deep gouges that we'd seen on the wrecked doors and in one place there were several holes in the ceiling. As I looked at those holes and wondered what had caused them, a pattern suddenly leapt into place. Three holes side by side and another behind; those were claw holes made by something hanging from the ceiling.

"Hey guys," I whispered, "make sure you keep a look above as well as all around huh." Everyone looked up and I noticed Ronjo's face pale by several more shades.

"Shit," Luggs hissed as he looked up. "What the fuck have we gotten ourselves into here?" Just as I was about to make a remark we were all silenced by a screech from somewhere above. As one we all looked up and listened, holding our breaths. Another screech and then a human cry that made even Luggs gasp in shock. Someone was dying horribly somewhere above us and from what we'd already seen, we knew what they were going through at that moment. Several shots rang out, accompanied by shouts that grew gradually fainter told us one of the groups was now down to two and that those two were running for their lives. "Oh for fuck's sake," Luggs said as he wiped a hand over his head. "I'm a co pilot on a two bit passenger liner. I shouldn't be dealing with this shit on what I get paid." He was right and I understood perfectly how he felt and nodded.

"Yeah well I'm just a law enforcement guy," I replied, "and I'm happy to deal with murderers and crazies anytime over this shit.

Come on, let's get this going before we lose what nerve we have left huh?" Luggs took a deep breath and rolled his neck around before nodding and stepping forward.

By the time we found ourselves back at the stairs, we'd found several more bodies and all but two of the remaining offices were torn to pieces. We were about to start down the stairs when we heard footsteps above and looked up to see Flark and the elderly guy coming towards us. They both looked white as sheets and the elderly guy had large sweat stains under his arms.

Where's Meesha?" Luggs asked. "We heard it all going on."

"We lost her," Flark sighed.

"Aww shit," Luggs replied. "What was it? We've seen the damage it does."

"It's like nothing you could imagine," Flark responded and the elderly guy nodded. "It's like a big bird but with teeth instead of a beak. It was waiting for us in one of the offices; just hanging from the ceiling and watching us for over a minute before it dropped down onto us."

"We had no idea it was there," the elderly guy gasped. "It was just hanging there, silent as the grave and watching us. Oh shit I'm too old for this."

"Take it easy Kitt," Flark soothed. "You've done great so far, don't lose it yet okay?" So that was his name huh? Kitt. He didn't look like a Kitt to me but then you can never really tell and I was pondering what name he did look like when we heard more footsteps coming down from the top floor. We were then joined by the military guy, the plain woman and the blue eyed plank pilot. All looked scared out of their wits but all were alive. So we'd made our tour of the central building with just one loss and we'd identified one of the creatures. It seemed we'd done okay, for now. "Let's get back downstairs, do the ground floor, get the kids and go find somewhere to hole up as base camp." Flark suggested and everyone nodded.

We started down the stairs but Flark suddenly stopped and turned to me. "Oh by the way Sam, we have a new problem too."

"We do?" I replied, wondering what the fuck else could be worse than this.

"Yeah I'm afraid so. Kitt here went to take a piss before we started and found your prisoner gone," he looked at the old guy who nodded and shrugged apologetically. Oh shit, this was just what we didn't need.

"What?" I yelled a little more sharply than I should've done. "How the fuck did that happen? That's all we need right now. As if being stranded on some rock surrounded by creatures who want to snack on our insides isn't enough, we now have a murderer running loose around the place." This was going from bad, to worse, to unbelievably shitty in quick succession and I was beginning to lose my temper.

"He's a murderer?" Ronjo asked.

"Yeah," Kitt replied, "so let's hope the creatures get him before he gets us huh?"

"Let's hope for that," I agreed without realising the significance of Kitt's remark. "He's not worth quite as much dead, but it shouldn't be a total loss."

We headed down the stairs and made a tour of the ground floor to find several more ransacked offices and just two more bodies. Then we all agreed that our next priority should be to find some place that offered us the means to make a drink and maybe even get something to eat. It took us no more than ten minutes to find the canteen where the office workers obviously took their breaks and I was delighted to see several nutri vend machines and an auto snack. Kitt and the young woman, who introduced herself as Marta le Roque, went to fetch the kids whilst I decided to go and check how Nembier got away. Cautiously I entered the bathroom and found the restraints lying on the floor undamaged. That was odd and I frowned as I checked them over; if he'd forced his way out of them there should be blood on them but they were clean. He must've somehow picked the locking mechanism and this just confused me even more. In all my years in this job I'd never known anyone pick these babies open, so the fact that Nembier had obviously managed it both enraged and intrigued me. Irritated, I sighed as I pocketed them and left the bathroom to head back to the canteen for a drink. Halfway there the scream rang out and I stopped dead in shock, momentarily startled out of my wits. It was a woman's scream and seemed to come from the general direction of the room where we'd hidden the two kids, Eddy and Jena. My hand automatically went to my hip and I unholstered my laser pistol as I ran towards the scream, to find Marta in the corridor with a hand over her mouth.

"What the fuck's happened?" I yelled. She closed her eyes and just shook her head. "Marta. What's happened?" I yelled again and shook her shoulder. She pointed into the room and I stepped gingerly towards the open doorway and peered in. The sound of murmuring voices met my ears and I recognised it as the old guy Kitt so I headed towards his voice. As I rounded the barricade we'd set up to hide the kids, I felt my stomach lurch and the breath leave my lungs. Kitt was trying to soothe his grandson Eddy and encourage him to move away from the remains of Jena who lay by his side, her head in his lap. The huge opening in her throat had sprayed blood for several feet and Eddy was saturated with it. "What the fuck did that?" I hissed at Kitt who ignored me as he continued soothing Eddy. "Kitt," I yelled, "what the fuck killed her?"

"How the fuck should I know," he snapped back.

"Well ask the kid, dammit."

"I'm trying you idiot, you'll have to be patient. He's scared out of his wits. It'll take time for him to tell me what happened."

"Hey kid," I barked and stepped forward. "What happened to her huh? Come on, tell us what happened. Hey kid are you listening to me?"

"That won't do any good Sam," Kitt hissed. "He's deaf and mute."

Now I understood why Kitt seemed to be gesturing at him all the time; he was using some kind of sign language with him. Then I remembered when we'd put the kids in here and how I'd seen Kitt gesturing at Eddy and how Ronjo seemed confused, no, shocked as he'd watched and I made a mental note to ask him about that. We became aware of the sound of running footsteps and soon Flark and the others entered the room and gasped in shock at the sight of Jena. Before I forgot, I went to look for Ronjo and found him outside, comforting Marta.

"Hey buddy. Y'know when we put the kids in there, before we set out to reccy the place?" He nodded. "I saw you watching Kitt as he did that sign language stuff with Eddy."

"So?"

"So I saw you suddenly look confused or shocked at something. Do you remember that?" He hesitated just a little too long before shaking his head and I knew he was lying. "Well buddy, if you do remember, I'd sure like to know what it was you were shocked about cos there may be a chance that our survival depends upon it okay?" He just looked at me so I glared at him for a few seconds before turning away, confident in the knowledge that he now knew that I knew he'd lied to me and I hoped that this knowledge would encourage him to open up. This situation was rapidly going down the shitter and I was beginning to realise that I was not in control of my destiny any more and that both scared and annoyed me. Adrenaline coursed through me, so I closed my eyes and leaned against the wall as I took deep breaths to try to calm myself down. Being stuck in this hell hole, surrounded by monsters with a penchant for people's innards, with a bunch of civilians and just two useful ex military guys on whom I could depend was bad enough but then within the first hour of getting here I'd lost Nembier and two of our group had been killed. Apart from the obvious, I was already aware that something wasn't adding up quite right about this situation and it irritated the fuck out of me that I didn't know what it was.

Kitt eventually persuaded Eddy to let him take him to the bathroom to clean up, so the rest of us headed back to the canteen. The thought of all those bodies that surrounded us worried me; not because I'm squeamish or anything but because I guessed the smell of all the blood and guts would be an attractant to the creatures outside. Why no one else had thought about this amazed me but then I reminded myself that these folks are just civilians and don't have the kind of common sense that fifteen years in this business has given me. A tap on my shoulder made me jump and I turned to find the dark skinned military guy standing behind me.

"Hey buddy. We haven't been properly introduced. I'm Sgt Simmia, 43rd Garrison, Unit Seventeen, Hecklorian Defence Corps.

Pleased to make your acquaintance." He extended his hand and shook my own.

"Sam Sinclair," I replied with a nod. "Freelance Law Enforcer, Tagged. I'm real pleased to meet you buddy. I'm beginning to feel lost here amongst these civilians. By the way do you have a first name or would you prefer me to call you Sergeant?"

"Oh sorry, the name's Dexter. I'm originally from Earth but my family emigrated to Heckloria when I was eight after my uncle married a Hecklorian woman. Call me Dex."

"Good to meet you Dex. I'm from Sigma Prime."

"Sam, can I ask you something in confidence?" he whispered suddenly and leaned in towards me and I nodded conspiratorially. "Am I the only one who thinks we should maybe clean the place up a little? You know, the bodies I mean. It makes me more than a little uncomfortable knowing they're just lying all around us and the smell must be like a dinner siren going off for those things out there. Surely it would make sense to get rid of em? Put em outside or something or even burn em maybe. What do you think?"

Well, to say I was relieved would be putting it mildly; I was so happy that someone was thinking along the same life preserving lines as me, I could've kissed the guy. Being in this situation was bad enough but being here surrounded by nice but useless survivalists made me think I'd been given the bum's rush, so the fact that Dex was now mirroring my own thoughts was both a relief and a delight. My relief must've showed as he smiled when I nodded frantically.

"Hell yeah I agree with you. We should definitely get them outside as soon as possible. Animals work off smell don't they? I know that hunchbacked thing that almost got us at the shuttle has bad eyesight so it obviously uses smell or sound or both to compensate. Besides, it's better to be safe than sorry huh?" Dex nodded and I was pleased I had one ally on whom I could depend. For the first time since landing in this hell, I thought just maybe I might survive. This lifted my spirits a little so I decided that as no one else had taken the lead, I might as well, so I spoke up.

"Hey guys can I have everyone's attention for a minute? Guys? Hello, guys please. Thanks. Umm my name is Sam Sinclair and I'm a Tagged Freelance Law Enforcer. I used to be in the military and I've been in law enforcement for fifteen years now and although I've not been in exactly this situation before, I'm clued up about survival techniques and have had to live by my wits on one or two occasions. My pal here is a Sergeant in the military and he and I have been discussing what's happening here and we both agree that if we're going to remain here any longer, we need to clean this place up." Murmurs went around the group and I groaned inwardly; this wasn't going to be easy.

"Well hey honey, I'll fetch you a broom," Luggs retorted and everyone grinned.

"Very funny," I glared; disappointed that as ex military himself, he should know better. "Now listen you idiot. All of those corpses with their guts hanging out will be giving off a very distinctive and inviting smell and every meat eater for hundreds of miles will be on their way for a free feast. Me and Dex here know that we should move the bodies outside of this building to help ensure our own safety." The grins had dropped from the faces now and I sighed inwardly as the truth of my words began to sink in.

"He's right," Luggs suddenly announced. "My apologies Sam. All that blood will be sending out a very clear signal and we'd be fools not to do something about it." His quick apology shocked me and I again found myself contrite at the speed at which I initially judged him by his appearance. Shit, I was beginning to like the guy.

"I agree," Flark joined in, "and although I only have authority over the shuttle crew amongst you, I would urge everyone to agree that this should be our next task."

"Why can't we just get back to the shuttle and leave?" Ronjo asked all of a sudden and my heart sank. It was too soon for this question and I hoped that the revelation the answer would bring could be delayed until we'd at least made ourselves relatively safe and comfortable here.

"Because the liner isn't due back here for three days and the shuttle doesn't have enough fuel to maintain an orbit for that long," Flark explained.

"Then why don't we call them up on the comms?" Marta cut in.

"They're already out of range of the shuttle comms," the blue eyed plank pilot replied. "The shuttle isn't designed for the long haul so there's no need for it to have long range comms. I'm afraid we're stuck here until the liner returns so we have to make the place as safe as we can."

"I really don't think I could face handling the bodies," Ronjo admitted. "I'm really sorry but I'm not military or anything and although as a minister of religion I'm used to dealing with the dead, actually handling mutilated corpses isn't really part of my resume. I'm more than willing to do anything else though to make up for it; you have only to ask."

"That's okay Ronjo. You'll pull your weight buddy, don't worry and thanks for your honesty," I smiled and couldn't help but admire the way he was handling this situation. That smile was also for me as I gave myself another pat on the back for the way I'd expertly summed him up earlier. He was obviously not a man of action so I'd labelled him as thinker guy and now I knew why; he was religious. "Does anyone else object?" I threw out the question, hoping no one would say yes and sighed with relief when no one did. "Okay then I reckon we should start at the top and work our way down. Ronjo, since you can't do the dirty work, perhaps you'd stay here and keep Eddy company and maybe keep up a supply of hot drinks for us?"

"Of course, I can do that," he nodded, "and I'll see if I can come up with some buckets so the floors can be sluiced down to at least try and wash away the blood. There may even be some cleaning chemicals hidden somewhere around, this place must've employed cleaners don't you think?"

"May I ask a question?" Marta cut in and everyone looked at her. She reddened a little but held her head up defiantly. "The bodies are all torn to pieces, with their guts hanging out and everything. Could we maybe find something to wrap them in first? I don't fancy having to carry armfuls of people's guts down four flights of stairs." Everyone nodded and I have to admit, the thought didn't exactly excite me either.

"There must be tablecloths or something around here," Cap replied as he went to a door at the rear of the canteen, "or bin liners; anything to make the job easier. Hey look here guys." We all rushed over to find a large storeroom containing all sorts of stuff, including a huge pile of tablecloths.

"Fantastic," I sighed, happy that at last something was going right for us. "Okay folks, grab a couple each and we'll leave the rest of the pile at the foot of the stairs." My smile turned to a frown as I turned to see Ronjo looking upset. "Ronjo? What's up buddy?"

"I'm sorry guys, it's just that to put them outside to be eaten by those things just seems a little, well a little, well y'know?"

"Yeah I know," I nodded. It seemed just a little callous to me too but this situation demanded we act to preserve our own lives and sentimentality would get in the way. Then I had an idea. "Would you feel happier if maybe, as a minister, you said a few words before we begin?" He brightened immediately and I noticed Dex wink at me for my quick thinking.

"Yes I would feel better," he nodded, "if everyone would be okay with it."

We gathered at the bottom of the stairs and Flark called for quiet. Ronjo spoke quietly but his voice was unwavering as he beseeched and his wisdom found its way into all of our hearts. I'm not a particularly religious guy but I do believe in some greater consciousness somewhere that hopefully knows the content of my character and my heart and I do hope for an afterlife of some sort when I die.

"Almighty Creator, we ask that you open your arms and receive the souls of all those of your children who passed from this life here in this place. We ask that the pain and torment of their passing be forgotten as they travel to whatever afterlife they seek for themselves and we ask forgiveness for that which we are about to do to their bodily remains. What we do is not done in anger or disrespect, but with hope that these lives that are left may continue until you see fit to bring them home to your side. Amen." Marta dabbed at her eyes and I smiled as I noticed Luggs sniff loudly and wipe his eyes on his sleeve.

"Thanks Ronjo," I smiled. "Nice words buddy." He nodded back in thanks. "Okay folks let's get it done shall we? All stick together now and we should be finished before you know it." We climbed the stairs once again and worked our way around the offices methodically. It was a fairly quick job and we got the top floor done in twenty five minutes. We took a moment to stretch our backs before heading down to the next floor and the process began again. Two hours later we headed back down to the ground floor to find Ronjo and Eddy sorting out buckets and chemicals he'd found.

"Eddy and I found a second storage room through the back of the canteen," he told us proudly. "We have a dozen buckets and enough of this chemical to float the Sally B."

"Great job guys," Flark responded. "Who wants to volunteer to sluice the floors down?" he looked around and three hands went up. The blue eyed plank pilot, Marta and Kitt grabbed the buckets and headed back up to the top floor.

"I'll ferry the containers of chemical up," Ronjo offered as he grabbed a couple and started to climb. My back was sore and I was longing to sit and relax but I grabbed three and headed after him. We divided the containers between the four floors and I did a quick mental calculation. There was more than enough so I urged them to be generous with it and headed back down to help clear the ground floor. Luckily there were only two more bodies and we had them out within ten minutes. Once the whole group were gathered back in the canteen, exhausted and dirty with blood, Ronjo surprised me again with his resourcefulness.

"Eddy and I also found some overalls in the store room so anyone who needs to, can change their clothes."

"Great job Ronjo," I nodded as I took one and held it up. "Anyone with blood on them should change, just to be safe. They're not glamorous but we're trying to stay alive here okay. Marta, you can use the bathroom first." She nodded and grabbed an overall and left the room. Ronjo made hot drinks and broke into the auto snack and we had ourselves a veritable feast. It was only as I was beginning to relax that I suddenly realised Nembier was still at large here somewhere and Marta was in the bathroom alone. My drink crashed to the floor as I leapt up.

"What's up Sam?" Dex asked.

"Oh shit," I hissed. "I forgot about Nembier and Marta has gone to the bathroom on her own." Dex's dark brown skin visibly paled a couple of shades and together the two of us raced from the canteen and headed for the bathroom. My heart was in my throat by the time we got there and I almost went rushing in but Dex stopped me just as I reached for the handle, so I banged on the door and yelled. "Marta, are you okay in there honey?"

"Yes I'm fine thanks," came the reply. "Why what's up?"

"Jeez thank god for that," Dex sighed and I nodded.

"Dex and I are gonna wait out here for you, just to make sure you're safe okay? Don't worry. Take your time."

We worked out a system so that everyone who left the main group had a competent gun with them and within another hour, we were washed and changed and back in the canteen. We were exhausted but our spirits were surprisingly high considering what we'd all been through and as the sun came up we worked out a watch rota so that everyone could get some sleep safe in the knowledge that at least two guns were keeping an eye on things. My whole body ached but I settled down as comfortably as I could and decided that as soon as I woke up, I had to find Nembier again.

Six hours later I was awake and standing at the nutri vend with Dex, wondering what to choose. These machines offer various hot and cold foods and drinks but although the taste may be acceptable, the appearance is anything but. Whatever you choose, you get a coloured gelatinous goo that looks and feels disgusting, but if you close your eyes and ignore the feel of the stuff, the taste isn't all that bad, depending on your meal choice of course. There's one on my ship and I live off the stuff for months at a time.

"So what's it to be Dex?" I asked. "Most of it will taste pretty okay, although I wouldn't recommend the Yamelian Pie to anyone but my most hated enemy." He laughed and nodded and I knew that as a soldier, he'd know all about the nutri vend and this infamous substance. Yamelian Pie is famous galaxy wide as being the most disgusting substance known and no one I'd ever met liked it, but still those damn nutri vends insist on offering it. "Y'know I'd like to end my life having met just one person who actually likes that muck. Do you think I'll get my wish Dex?"

"Not a chance in hell Sam," he laughed and I was forced to agree; the chances of that happening were slim to none. As we ate, we discussed our situation and traded ideas as to how we might improve our chances and better our living standards. Suddenly Flark entered with the blue eyed plank, panting as though they'd been running.

"Well we now know how the creatures were able to get across the trench," Flark announced and everyone looked up. "It was Chip here who saw it first," he indicated the blue eyed plank pilot. "Chip?"

"Yeah well umm, it seems as though a landslide filled in part of the trench over at the north end and formed a sort of bridge, enabling the creatures to cross. I was on the top floor scoping out the area through one of the windows and saw it. I could even see a couple of those hunchback things strolling across it."

"What about the flying ones?" Ronjo cut in. "How the hell did they keep those out?"

"We can answer that too," Flark said as he spread out the plans of the complex and pointed to a small square on the perimeter of the island. "It seems that this hut is actually an entrance to an underground room that contains the power grid for the whole Island. It has a mag field antenna on the top of it, which collects power from the planet's magnetic field and uses it to power the complex. It's an old fashioned system but reliable and gives an unending supply of power directly from the planet itself. A lot of these types of communities still use the system. Anyway, the antenna has probably broken, cutting off the power grid but more importantly, cutting off the laser shielding net."

"Umm, can you say that again in layman's terms," Marta asked apologetically.

"Sorry, yeah of course," Chip said as he flashed her a smile. "There is a net of laser beams in a dome that covers the whole island, to keep out the flying creatures I guess. When the antenna broke, the power to this net shut down, allowing the creatures through." He gave her another smile and she nodded.

"But we're not without power," Ronjo said. "We have some lights working and the nutri vend and auto snack are still operative."

"There's bound to be a system of back up generators somewhere," I offered. "We're obviously running off some kind of emergency power system in here."

"Umm, I'm sorry to put a dampener on things," Marta said suddenly, "but something has been bothering me. This may be a silly question but umm, how did that creature get into this part of the building?" Silence ensued as we all turned the question over in our minds. "When we arrived," she continued, "the main door was closed and we've not discovered a single broken or open window, so how did it get in? Don't you think we need to find out before more come in the same way?" My heart sank as the truth of her words hit home. Just as I was getting to the point of believing that all we had to do was find something to occupy our minds until the Sally B returned to rescue us, we were back with the realisation that we could all still be eaten alive.

"She's right," I said, breaking the tense silence at last. "We must find how and where it got in, even if it just means we know which part of the building to avoid, but we have to find out. And I have to recapture Nembier too, especially now he has another murder on his hands." Everyone looked at me in shock and I sighed. "Jena Marks' body wasn't in the same state as all the other bodies here, and if she was killed by one of those things, how come Eddy was unhurt? No, it must've been Nembier. The only thing I can't for the life of me understand is why he would kill her." Everyone ate the remainder of their tasteless lunch in silence as we pondered our coming mission.

Okay folks I'm going to break the report here temporarily. I'm getting a bit dry mouthed with all this talking so I'm going to get something to eat and I have to change this vidicom lens too. V-log reference AZ267/M, data log reference point 2458712/6541.

CHAPTER FOUR

Hang on a second while I readjust this new vidicom lens. There was an unfortunate incident a couple of weeks ago when umm, oh never mind that's another story. Okay there we go, now where was I? Oh yeah, V-log reference AZ267/M continuing report. Data log reference point 2458712/6542.

Well as I said earlier, we all ate our lunch pretty quietly and I think all of us were further unsettled when we realised we had to go searching for how and where the creatures gained entry to the prison and I was more than a little irritated that I also was to be chasing Nembier all over again. At least we all knew we weren't going to have to search the upper floors again, which narrowed things down quite a bit but it also meant we couldn't avoid venturing into the cell wings. This was something I was hoping we wouldn't need to do, but we all knew there was nowhere else to go looking without going outside so we decided to split up into two groups this time. This would help ensure safety as much as possible and cut down the time it would take us to search all eight cell wings. We tried to steal ourselves for the carnage we fully expected to find in the cells, but then something occurred to me.

"Y'know guys," I said as we prepared to split up into two groups, "the prisoners down in the cells might not actually be dead." Blank stares greeted me alongside several frowns so I sighed deeply and explained as clearly as I could. "Prison cells are constructed tough. They are designed to keep folks inside, not to be easily broken out of, or into. We could find the prisoners still alive down there. Still alive and hungry and then we'll have the added complication of taking care of them." Dex and Flark looked decidedly annoyed at this.

"Shit," Dex exclaimed as he looked at me, "you're right Sam. And there could be another problem too. We could find some of them still confined, as you say but some could've gotten out and be roaming around down there. We could find ourselves surrounded by who knows how many murderers and crazies."

"Look, maybe we should just stay right out of it," Marta said, her faltering voice giving away her fear. It scared all of us and I felt sorry for her but at the same time, I had to get Nembier back. Call me a gold digger if you want, but a guy has to live you know.

"We can't ignore it Marta," the blue eyed plank suddenly cut in as he went and put an arm around her shoulder and gave her his best movie star smile. "We have to take a look and see where those creatures got in so we know where to concentrate our firepower tonight. I'll make sure you're okay honey, you stick with me huh? Besides, Sam here is law enforcement and he'll make sure they're no danger to us."

My irritation rose several notches and I almost slapped him for that last remark before realising that he was right; everyone would be expecting me to be able to make sure not one of the hundreds of crazies and murderers held in this place would harm them, just because I had a couple of sets of handcuffs and a tag. Closing my eyes, I sighed deeply as I realised the weight my job put on my shoulders.

Once I felt calm I glanced at Ronjo and was surprised to see him checking the gun I'd given him the night before. "Ronjo, do you want to sit this out and do Eddy duty again?" I asked but he shook his head.

"No. Thanks for asking but I want to stop being such an old woman for a change. I'm gonna tag along on this one if that's okay."

"That's great buddy, glad to have you along," I grinned and he nodded. It's amazing how people find reserves of strength and courage in a crisis that they never knew they possessed.

"I'll stay with Eddy this time," Kitt said as he took the boy's hand. "I'm too old and slow to deal with those creatures anyway. I'd just hold you back and put you all in danger. We'll stay here and tidy up a bit." Flark nodded and I guessed he must've felt a little relieved not to have to baby the old guy again.

"Okay so let's split up into two groups huh?" Flark suggested. "Make sure each group has an equal number of competent guns okay?"

Dex, Ronjo, Luggs and me set off towards the rear end of the building and I was pleased to have these guys in my group. There was no doubt in my mind that I'd got the best of the bunch and I felt pretty confident that we could deal with whatever came our way. The only potential weak link was Ronjo but I had to admit that he was trying his best not to be a burden. A large open space occupied the central core of the building; a short corridor at the far end leading to a small security station that guarded the entrance to the cell wings. A desk and computer console stood at one side, behind which we could see eight security vidicom screens, none of which seemed to be operational. Beyond the desk, eight doors led off in different directions, forming a semicircle like the rays of a sun in a kid's painting. The doors were numbered one to eight from left to right. My group opted for the first four and left five through to eight for Flark's group. Flark had a set of restraints just in case he should catch up with Nembier and I had another set in my own pocket.

To my surprise, the doors weren't locked and swung open with just a push. Frowning, I looked at Dex, who shrugged and shouldered his laser rifle. We stepped through into a short corridor that stretched before us and disappeared down a flight of steps. We approached the steps and peered into the gloom but could see nothing. Luggs got out a flashlight and we all groaned aloud at the sight that greeted us at the foot of the short flight of steps. The remains of the door to cell wing number one lay strewn at the bottom of the steps; each piece graffitied with deep gouges and spattered with blood.

"Bingo," Dex hissed.

"Shit," I replied.

"Oh fuck," Luggs added and Ronjo gasped.

"Is there a light switch anywhere?" Luggs asked as he examined the outside of the doorway. Before anyone could reply he found a sensor plate covered in blood and smacked his hand onto it. The cell block leapt into view before us and we found ourselves staring at half a dozen sleeping creatures as they hung from the ceiling. The sudden explosion of light woke them up and we had just seconds to register what was about to happen. Dex and his military training gained my eternal admiration as he switched into autopilot, closely followed by ex military Luggs and the two of them opened fire. The cell block erupted into shrieks as the creatures found themselves under fire and dropped from the ceiling and headed towards us. They were basically bird like but their wings had skin stretched across instead of feathers and their claws were easily six inches long. Instead of a beak, they had a normal mouth with a pair of long curved fangs hanging down over the bottom lip. Another matching pair curved up from the bottom jaw and overlapped the top lip; the two pairs interlocking and giving them the ability to rip and tear rather than cut and slice. Their eyes were huge and I knew there would be no way to hide from these night creatures with excellent eyesight. Roughly the height of a grown man, they were a formidable sight as they flew towards us, their jaws open much wider than one would think normal.

Fear brought me to action and I raised my rifle, joining my fire to that of Dex and Luggs. Within a few seconds I faintly registered a body squeezing between me and Luggs; the pop, pop, pop that followed telling me that Ronjo had found his mojo at last and was bravely standing with us, his AB11 Rookie useless against these monsters. At the speed they were flying, it would take no more than five or six seconds for them to close the gap between us and we knew we had nowhere to go to outrun them. We had no choice but to stand and fight, so we stood our ground and gave them all we had. One by one they fell until the last of them landed less than a foot from our boots. For several seconds we stood unmoving; the sudden silence deafening. As my mind began to calm I became aware of laboured breathing beside me and turned to see Dex and Luggs, staring into space as I had no doubt just been doing myself. Ronjo was shaking, his Rookie still held out in front of him, ready to fire so I put a hand on his arm and talked him out of his shock.

"Ronjo, it's okay. You did fantastic buddy, well done and thank you. They're all done now, you can relax. That's it, lower the gun. Good job," I encouraged and slowly he blinked and lowered the weapon. "Dex? Luggs? You both okay guys?" Both sighed and blinked several times as they came to their senses and nodded. "Well done guys, we have a good team huh?"

"The best," Dex nodded as he turned and grinned at me. "Okay let's see what we have inside."

Two hundred and fifty cells on each side of the long corridor stretched out before us and all were eerily silent. We crept forward, all of us now needing no reminding to look up as well as all around and approached the first of the cells.

"Dex, Luggs, you guys keep watch all around okay? Ronjo, you check the cells on that side and I'll check these ones. That sound okay?" Grunts responded immediately and we continued on. My heart sank as we reached the first of the cells and I saw the laser fences had gone down. "Shit," I hissed and everyone looked at me. "The cells use a laser fence system which obviously runs off the same power grid as the safety net that keeps the flying creatures out. With the antenna down, the laser fences will have come down, letting the inmates out and the creatures in."

"Dammit," Dex hissed with a loud sigh. "How much fucking worse can this get?"

"Ronjo," I whispered. "You better prepare yourself buddy cos we're undoubtedly gonna be finding the remains of the inmates somewhere around." His eyes widened and his face paled. He gritted his jaw and nodded at me. "I just thought you ought to be prepared okay? If you need to leave, that's all right."

"I'll be fine Sam," he replied with as much defiance as he could muster, which wasn't much but I couldn't help but admire him. "I'll be fine."

We worked our way along the corridor and each cell held at least one body. Some lay on their bunks as if asleep but all bore the same injuries as the ones we'd seen upstairs; the abdomen split open and the contents wrenched out in an untidy heap leaving us wondering how all of that stuff could fit into that small space. The floor was awash with blood and the metallic smell tainted the air, making us all retch by the time we reached the end of the corridor to find the emergency exit door standing open.

"So here's one way they're getting in," Dex said as he pulled the huge heavy metal door closed and struggled with the cross lever that held it shut. "Help me with this would ya?" Luggs put his weight to it and together, the two of them secured the door. "Thanks buddy, that's one down, three more to go."

We jogged back along the corridor and up the steps to the central hall to find Kitt and Eddy standing there with a tray of cold drinks.

"Oh my god you're okay," he sighed with relief. "I heard shots and then it went quiet for ages. I was just beginning to wonder if me and Eddy were alone here. We've made some cold drinks for everyone, thought you might need them. Here, help yourselves."

"Man are we ever glad to see you," Luggs smiled as he helped himself to a drink.

"You obviously got some creatures down there too then?" Kitt asked and Dex nodded.

"What do you mean us too?" I asked.

"I heard shots from that corridor too," he said as he pointed to door number five. "They started shooting a few seconds after you did, but they're not back yet."

"Maybe we should go and," Ronjo began but just then the door opened and Flark stumbled out, swiftly followed by Cap, the blue eyed plank and then Marta. All dropped to their knees and heaved deep breaths. Marta was visibly shaking as Kitt went up and handed drinks around.

"Oh god," she whispered, "I've never been so terrified in all my life. They were down there, hanging from the ceiling and just came for us as soon as we switched the light on." The blue eyed plank reached out and took her hand and gave it a squeeze and she did her best to smile.

"Yeah, same with us," I replied. "We found the emergency door at the end was standing open. I'm guessing that when the laser fences went down, the inmates decided to let themselves out, little realising that they were signing their own death warrants."

"Yeah, our door was open too," Flark nodded.

"Shit I would kill for a cigarette," I said. It's been five years or so since I've smoked regularly but under extreme stress I do find it calms me down. Not once had I seen any of my colleagues smoking so I guessed I'd be out of luck, but to my surprise, the blue eyed plank dug into his pocket and threw a pack over.

"Help yourself," he said, "and light one for me while you're at it would ya?"

After a short break we set off down to cell wing number two, leaving Flark and his group heading off to number six. As we got to the top of the short flight of steps that led down to the door, we stopped dead in our tracks with shock. The steps were littered with bodies, all torn open as before and it looked as if the inmates had been caught as they tried to enter the main building. We picked our way down through the bloody mass of bodies and Dex put his hand out towards the sensor pad that would bring the lights up. He looked at me and I held up three fingers, then two, then one and he slapped the sensor; bringing the whole of cell wing two into view. No creatures flew at us this time but the place was littered with corpses. We could see the door at the end of the corridor was closed so we assumed the inmates had either gone out that way, seen what was waiting for them and come back inside, only to be met with creatures that had entered through the other corridors, or they had simply chosen to enter the building rather than go outside. Either way they were doomed.

"Well it looks like this one is safe," Luggs said as he lowered his gun and turned to go.

"Wait a minute guys," I whispered before they could retrace their steps and leave me there. "I have to find Nembier remember? Wanna help me out here?" Dex nodded and indicated towards the light sensor.

"Okay Sam," he said loudly, "looks like this one's clear. Let's go try number three huh?" he grinned at me and slapped the sensor, sending the place into darkness once again. We all held our breath, not daring to make a noise and strained our ears. Just as I was about to speak, we all heard a noise to our left. A scuffling, accompanied by a grunt and murmurs of disgust, then footsteps. Dex slapped the sensor and light exploded into the corridor, momentarily blinding Nembier as he stood there red from head to toe in blood from the bodies he'd hidden himself beneath. He looked at me in shock as I took aim.

"Tell me why I shouldn't kill you, you annoying fuck," I yelled angrily at I took a step forward, gun aimed at his head. "Go on, tell me why." Dex and Luggs stepped forward, guns aimed at his chest and he dropped to his knees and began to sob. Still angry at him, I lowered my rifle and dug in my pocket for the restraints and approached him. "Professor Kluvak Nembier, I am restraining you once again in connection with nine murders on Agrillia 3 and also for the murder of Jena Marks here on Floxham 4." After I secured his wrists we marched him back along the corridor, still sobbing. Once at the central hallway I pushed him to the floor and despite my normal self control, I lost it and kicked him hard in the gut. He yelled in agony and crumpled into a heap. "She was just fourteen you sick fuck. Why in hell's name did you have to kill a child huh? What the fuck did she do to you?" My anger burst out of me, the frustration and fear this situation caused within me, fuelling its force and I went to kick him again but Luggs put a hand on my arm and shook his head.

"No Sam," he whispered and looked me right in the eyes.

"I didn't kill anyone," Nembier sobbed as he held his gut. "You have to believe me. I didn't kill anyone. Not home on Agrillia and not here either. I can't prove it but I didn't do it."

"Shut up you psycho fuck," I yelled as I grabbed him and hauled him to his feet before marching him back to the bathroom. Taking extra care, I secured him, this time with two sets of restraints, with both hands secured to different anchor points. By keeping his hands far apart, he'd not be able to pick the locking mechanism again.

"Please don't leave me in here alone Sam," he begged as I turned to leave and again, the vague feeling swept into my mind that made me momentarily wonder about him.

"If you're not here when I get back and I have to come looking for you again, I'll shoot you and bring you in dead next time." His gaze fell to the floor as I glowered at him and with the last of my frustration, I thumped the wall angrily before shutting and locking the door behind me. His loud sobs followed me as I marched away to rejoin my group.

Throwing all self control to the wind, I helped myself to another cigarette from the pack the blue eyed plank gave me and breathed in deeply to calm myself down. Before I finished it, door six opened and Flark and his group stumbled out coughing and retching. Without waiting to be asked, I lit another cigarette and handed it to the blue eyed plank, who took it and nodded at me. It turned out that they found a similar scene waiting for them in cell wing six as we'd found in number two and we all agreed that the inmates must've first used the emergency exit door, only to find themselves surrounded by creatures. When they had the sense to re enter the cell wing and close the heavy emergency doors, they must've thought themselves safe but what they couldn't know was that inmates from other cell wings had left their emergency doors open, allowing the creatures inside to wreak havoc. We knew we had to get all the emergency doors properly shut before anyone could relax.

"We're halfway through guys," I said to the exhausted group, "but we have to get the other four done before dark. Does anyone not want to continue?" I looked from one to the other and I will admit to assuming Marta and Ronjo might ask to sit out for a while but to my surprise no one spoke. "Okay, let's do this huh?" Dex nodded and I turned to walk towards door number three when Kitt came walking up with more drinks.

"Does anyone know why the door to the bathroom is locked? I can't get in there."

"Oh yeah sorry that's my fault," I said. "We found Nembier in number two and I've secured him in there again and locked the door this time. If he is able to get out of the restraints again, he'll have the door to get through too and maybe we'll be back from clearing these cell wings by that time so I can kick his ass before he gets away again. Come on, I'll let you in there before we do the next cell wing." He nodded and I followed him to the bathroom and unlocked the door. My whole body ached and I was so tired I could hardly stand as I stepped aside to let him enter first before following him inside. This was the first time since we got to Floxham that something happened that I can look back on in the cold light of day and realise was a huge clue, but at the time it was weird enough for me to notice and get me suspicious but I didn't see the whole picture. Nembier looked at Kitt as we entered and at first I didn't see anything strange. It wasn't until I was re locking the door as we left that I realised it was Nembier's expression as he looked at Kitt that was weird. It was almost a smile of recognition that flashed across his face and in any other circumstance I'd expect him to ask how he'd been since they last met. As soon as he saw me though, the look vanished and he was back to his normal expressionless self and kept his eyes to the floor. As I locked the door I finally had a little warning bell go off inside my head that I had no intention of ignoring. Although I didn't yet know why, I suddenly realised that I didn't want to trust Kitt anymore.

We headed towards cell wing three and approached the steps that led down to the door, which we could all see had been smashed to pieces. The lack of bodies on the steps told us what we didn't want to know and Dex and I exchanged a glance and a nod. He reached towards the sensor pad and looked back at me.

"Okay guys," I whispered. "Same procedure as in number one. Keep your heads and keep firing. Everyone ready?" Luggs adjusted his gun and nodded; his eyes staring into the gloom ahead, while Ronjo stared at me with scared eyes. "Okay Ronjo?" He nodded and raised his useless gun and I looked at Dex and nodded. "Let's go," I whispered as Dex slapped the sensor and all hell broke loose. It seemed as if the whole cell wing was filled with the shrieking creatures; the noise and flapping of their wings momentarily overwhelming us. We stood our ground in the doorway and fired as they soared towards us, dropping one by one as they closed the gap. As they reached the doorway they suddenly swooped around and away from our fire and headed back to the far end of the corridor and the open emergency door. For a moment I hoped they were intending to go back outside but at the last second they swooped around and headed back towards us for a second wave. Again we opened fire as they soared towards us; their screeching splitting the air painfully. The last one fell twenty feet from where we stood and we lowered our weapons as the silence enveloped us.

"Shit, oh shit," Dex exclaimed as he ran a hand through his hair and sighed, his dark brown skin enhancing the shine of sweat on his brow. Ronjo stood between Luggs and me; his arms still held out in front, weapon at the ready. Again, I gently put my hand on his arm.

"It's okay Ronjo," I soothed, "it's done. You did good. You did real well buddy, thank you for your help. Relax now okay?" He blinked a few times and lowered his arms as he sighed deeply. "Come on guys." I stepped forward, "let's get that door closed huh?" We ran to the end of the corridor and pulled the heavy door shut and locked the lever in place. It was as we leant on the door to get our breath back that we heard Ronjo's yell. We spun around and I found myself staring into a pair of gaping jaws; the two opposing sets of curved fangs yellowed with age and I noticed one of them had its sharpened tip missing. Time seemed to slow and then stop as first my hearing left me, then my vision narrowed until I was looking through a long tunnel with just that face at the end. The huge, soulless black eyes bored into mine as the head retracted, readying itself to strike forwards. The jaws opened even wider and I tried to come to terms with the fact that I was about to die as the head began its strike towards me. For as long as I live I will never forget the sight of that eye imploding a split second before the back of the skull exploded. The rest of the body came to rest against my legs and abdomen; the wings spread out sideways and behind like a grey leather cloak. Slowly, I looked up to see Ronjo still holding that ridiculous AB11 Rookie at arms length, his eyes wide.

As my senses returned, I was vaguely aware of shouts to the side but I was mesmerised by the sight of Ronjo and that useless gun that just saved my life. Slowly he turned his head to look at me, his eyes still wide with shock and I saw the trickle of blood that ran from one corner of his mouth and dripped off his chin. He coughed and spat blood everywhere and looked down at himself. Still trying to force myself to calm down, I followed his gaze and saw the gaping rent in his abdomen that he struggled to hold shut as his intestines slithered through his fingers and trailed down his legs.

"No," I yelled as I came to my senses and rushed to his side. "Ronjo, stay with us buddy." Cold gripped me through to the bone and I held onto his hand as he dropped to the floor spitting blood and gasping for air. My heart leapt in panic as I crouched down beside him and looked into his eyes as he held my gaze and died in agony. "You did real good buddy and I'm proud to have you on my team." He nodded slowly and his hand went limp in mine. For long moments I held onto his hand until I felt someone prying it from my grasp and reluctantly allowed Dex to steer me back along the corridor to the central hallway. Luggs was openly crying and I will admit I shed tears for the guy too. He was scared shitless but managed to conquer his fear and hold his own alongside the rest of us and he'd died saving my life and I felt like a shit leaving him down there amongst the dead prisoners.

"I don't wanna leave him down there amongst murderers and crazies," I said as I wiped my eyes and lit a cigarette with shaking hands. "I want to bring him back here so he can have a proper burial when this is over. He's a hero and deserves to be treated like one huh? Please?" No one argued with me and we all agreed to retrieve him when all the cell wings were cleared and made safe. Flark revealed that cell wing seven contained nine of the creatures, three of whom had fled out through the open emergency door when they'd started firing. Kitt handed round some cold drinks before we got up and readied ourselves for one final excursion, after which we could hopefully remain safe until the Sally B returned.

Luggs kicked the door to cell wing four open and thumped his fist on the wall in anger. "I hope you're ready for me down there cos I am gonna make you pay, assholes," he hissed. He taught me something about himself at that moment that I never expected to learn. He cared. This rough looking, course mouthed throwback with prehistoric eyebrow ridges cared deeply about people and had a moral code that even I'd be proud to have. As we headed towards cell wing four and whatever awaited us down there, I made a vow to myself that if we got out of this with our lives, I would keep in touch with Luggs and be proud to have him as a friend. Doing the job I do means I can't have buddies like other people do. It's impossible for me to go round and sit and have a beer in the evening; I can't make a date to go to a show with my friends or catch a holadau game at the weekends. You could say it's a lonely kind of job so I try not to make attachments of any kind; not just for my own sake but for the other person too. Having friends makes you responsible for them in some ways and I don't want to disappoint anyone by not being able to be there as a friend. It's far easier for me to keep some detachment, but I was determined to keep in touch with Luggs as I knew he was someone whose presence was of value to me.

We descended the steps and found the door to the cell wing still intact and closed. There were no bodies outside so we prepared ourselves for another battle. Luggs reached for the door and pushed but it held firm. He looked at me and frowned.

"It won't open," he hissed as he pushed again, giving it all his weight. "It's like it's wedged from the inside."

"What?" Dex frowned. "All of us together, come on." We all leaned against the door and shoved as hard as we could but it moved less than an inch. "What the fuck is holding it? I'm gonna switch on the light okay guys? Get ready." He slapped the sensor pad and the cell wing flooded with light. We peered through the window but something was blocking our view.

"What's all that shit in front of the door?" I said as I tried to peer through the gaps in the debris that we could see piled against the door.

"Search me," Luggs replied.

"But who could've," I began but something caught my eye off to the left of my field of vision. "Hey I just saw movement off to the left. Can either of you guys see?" Dex and Luggs peered in, then I noticed Luggs eyebrows raise in surprise.

"Shit, there's a guy walking around in there. There's someone alive."

"And there's two guys over this side too," Dex said.

"They're alive in there?" I couldn't believe this. "My god we have to let them know we've secured the place. They must be scared out of their wits."

"Should we?" Dex said suddenly. "They're prisoners remember. Murderers and who knows what other types of crazies are in there. Maybe we should let em keep on thinking it's safer for them to stay barricaded in there huh?"

"He has a point Sam," Luggs remarked and I had to admit that it was a valid point. This was more complications we really didn't need and I scratched my head as I mulled over the problem. By pure chance I just happened to glance to my left and notice a sign above the sensor pad that made me smile. "Hey look guys. Over there by the sensor pad, see? It says Cell Wing Four - Minimum Security Risk Protocol - Extended Light Privileges. That must mean there's no crazies in there, just petty thieves and stupid kids wanting to be tough."

"I guess the low risk guys get more light than the crazies," Dex remarked. "Well let's see if we can get their attention." He began banging on the door and yelling. We yelled at the tops of our voices and pretty soon a face appeared, eyes wide with suspicion. Then another and soon there was quite a crowd looking at us looking at them. Once we persuaded them it was safe, they began to dismantle their barricade and we were soon introducing ourselves to four hundred petty thieves and fraudsters. They told us that like everyone else, they first tried escaping via the emergency door but soon found that to be a very bad idea, so they ran back inside but found creatures had entered via other emergency doors. They decided to return here and barricade themselves in by using their bunks and bits and bobs of furniture from their cells. Once or twice they'd braved an excursion to the canteen for food and water but other than that, they'd remained alive this way for four days so far.

"We have the rest of this building secured now," I announced, "so you've no need to hide in here anymore. Before we go upstairs though, I must tell you that we have a woman among our group and a young boy who's deaf and mute so please be respectful."

A tall man with a dignified air about him stepped forward. "My name is Clavan Milgram and I embezzled money from the company I worked for. I was guilty and I got found out and sent here to pay for my crime. All of us here in this wing have done wrong but no one will come to harm from any one of us. We are thieves here Sir, not murderers or child molesters. Hopefully those have been dealt with by those creatures. No one is in danger from us, I give you my word."

"Then you're all welcome to come up and join us," I smiled and shook his hand. "I need to tell you though, that I'm a Freelance Law Enforcer and I have a prisoner with me under restraint. He's accused of murder, but my job is to take him in, not to make a judgement about his guilt or innocence. Is that gonna be a problem for anyone?"

"Who did he kill?" a small thin man asked.

"He's accused of killing nine scientists on Agrillia 3 and there is a possibility that he killed a teenage girl here at the prison, although I'm no longer convinced of his guilt on that," I replied and noticed Dex and Luggs look at me surprised.

"You're not?" Dex asked.

"I thought it was cut and dried," Luggs said.

"So did I," I nodded, "but something happened that makes me think differently now. I'll tell you all about it later okay. Let's get back and introduce our new friends here to the guys upstairs."

CHAPTER FIVE

Flark and his group were more than a little surprised to see Dex, Luggs and I return with four hundred inmates and Marta's eyes widened in fear when she found herself surrounded by so many men. A wave of pity flushed through me so I made a point of introducing her to Clavan.

"Marta, this here is Clavan Milgram. He has assured me that you have no need to be scared okay? You'll be safe here. He's promised me." Clavan smiled and extended a hand, which she shook with a nervous smile. A silent prayer filtered out from my mind in the hope that he hadn't been lying to me; I had no desire to look like a total idiot after finding her gang raped by four hundred sex starved inmates.

"I give you my word," Clavan assured her, "that no one amongst us will be any danger to you, or anyone here. Most of us are petty thieves and many of us have families; wives and children whom we look forward to getting back to once our terms are finished. Most of us in wing four have less than a year still to serve until we gain our freedom and none of us has any desire to earn more time here." Marta nodded and gave another nervous smile and despite only having met the guy a few minutes earlier, I felt sure he was on the level. Like I said before, I like to think I'm an excellent judge of character and I just knew I wasn't wrong this time.

The next two jobs on my list were to retrieve Ronjo's body and see to Nembier so I excused myself and went to the canteen store room in search of another pair of the overalls Ronjo had found the night before. While there I also found the remaining stack of tablecloths so I grabbed a couple and headed back to where the group still sat in the central hallway, talking and getting to know each other.

"Hey guys," I called and all eyes looked at me. "A buddy of mine gave his life to save me down in cell wing three, and I don't wanna leave him down there. Can I have a couple of volunteers to help me retrieve him?" At least forty men stood and I was touched at their readiness to help. "Thanks guys," I smiled and led the way down into cell wing three. It seemed weird being back down here in the silence, surrounded by so many dead and it did creep me out a bit. My hands instinctively balled into fists as I kept my eyes fixed on the body I could see at the far end and marched right up to him. The floor was awash with blood and I felt the cold wetness seep through my pant leg as I knelt down by his side and spread out a couple of the tablecloths. My eyes began to well up as I put a hand on his chest. "Thanks buddy, you're a hero, you know that?" We got him wrapped up as best we could and carried him back up and laid him down by the main entrance door alongside the remains of Meesha Roddry and Jena Marks.

My next task was to see to Nembier, so I grabbed the overalls and unlocked the bathroom. His eyes widened as he saw me enter and he drew his knees up and tried to scuffle out the way; afraid I was going to kick him again I guess. After locking us both in I fished for my keys and let him out of the restraints. He looked a little surprised to be let free but stayed sitting on the ground, obviously mistrustful of me and I have to admit that I felt bad at having lost my rag with him earlier. I've always prided myself on doing my job properly and to know that I lost it and behaved like a low life Merc, made me feel ashamed.

"Take off those clothes and have a wash," I said; trying to make it sound like a friendly offer rather than an order. "Here's a pair of clean overalls to put on so you can be clean and comfortable." He hesitated for a moment so I stepped back and leant against the door and lit myself another of the blue eyed plank's cigarettes. "It's okay, go on," I coaxed. "Look buddy, I'm sorry I lost it earlier okay? I shouldn't have done that and I apologise and I will add a note to my report about it, so you've no need to feel you're being bullied. I may be a law enforcement guy but I do have a code y'know, even if I can't always stick to it." He seemed pacified by my admittance so he stood and began to remove his clothes. Shock and shame enveloped me as my eyes registered his badly bruised gut that obviously gave him some pain. "I'll see if there's any painkillers around here for you."

He turned the tap and waited for the basin to fill. "I didn't do it Sam," he said quietly. "I haven't killed anyone. I can't prove it though."

"It's not my job to judge you," I replied before realising that by attacking him earlier, I'd done just that, "and I'm sorry I hurt you earlier. For what it's worth though, between you and me, I don't think you killed the girl yesterday. Don't ask me how I know, but I don't think you did it."

"Thank you for your honesty," he said as he began to wash, "and in return, I'll offer you something." This caught me by surprise and he smiled for the first time. "Want to know how I got out of those restraints yesterday?" I nodded. "I didn't escape them by myself you know Sam. I'm not an expert lock picker. I'm a scientist who gets his rocks off by studying ancient languages scrawled onto stones. Killing doesn't excite me Sam and I get no thrill from the chase. Ancient ruins are what give me a hard on my friend. I'm the ultimate boring old fart; happiest when I'm crawling around in some dusty ruin, gazing at scratches on stones. I've never been in the military, never learned to fly, never been married nor had any children and I've made love seven times in all of my sixty two years of life. One talent I do have though is an excellent memory and I never forget a face."

"So why are you telling me all this, and what's it got to do with how you got out of the restraints?" I asked, bemused but very interested.

"Because the person who let me out of them is someone I've seen before." This was the last thing I'd expected to hear and my shock must've been obvious because he smiled again.

"And who is that?"

"Well Sam, that's the first question that needs an answer."

"And what would that answer be?"

"You'll find that by asking the second question." Now he was being cryptic and I was getting annoyed. He was getting one over on me but I couldn't blame the guy for playing this little game. How the fuck was I to know who let him out of the restraints and more importantly, why? Ahh, now the penny was beginning to drop so I smiled triumphantly.

"And why would this unknown person want to let you out of the restraints?"

"Well done Sam," he sniggered. "You're good. You're very good."

I thought about what little I knew of Nembier. He's an Agrillian scientist who, by his own admission, gets his rocks off by studying ancient languages and hasn't been laid in years. He may not be the life and soul of the party but he's bound to be pretty well connected, amongst the scientific community anyway. He could be well travelled and for all I knew, he could have friends and contacts from many worlds. How was I to know who he was talking about? I hadn't the faintest idea but I knew I had to find out. Even though it's not strictly my job to find out information about the crimes my cargo may be accused of, this had got to me and for my own peace of mind, I had to know. I didn't know where to begin to answer these cryptic questions though and it showed.

"So where do you go from here now you have this news huh?" he asked with a grin. I shrugged and ran a hand through my hair. "Well answer me this Sam. How much do you know about Agrillian law and social history?"

"Practically nothing," I admitted as he dressed, "but I'm going to find out. Now come on, I'm taking you to the canteen so you can be more comfortable. We found some inmates alive by the way, so I'm gonna be putting a team on watching you twenty four seven. That way you don't have to sit in here on your own and you can have something to eat and drink but I meant what I said earlier though, if I have to chase you all over this place once more, I'll put you outside and leave you to the creatures okay?"

"I'll not try to escape Sam," he said and extended his wrists towards me. "It wasn't my idea last time remember." He locked eyes with me as I cuffed him and unlocked the door.

Back in the canteen I led him over to the nutri vend and helped him get some food and a drink and sat him down at a corner table. Everyone was eating and talking after the terrifying afternoon we'd had and I felt bad interrupting but it was necessary.

"Hey guys," I called and waited for the chatter to die down. "Sorry to interrupt again. Now, for the benefit of our new friends here, this guy here is Professor Kluvak Nembier. He's under restraint because he's wanted in connection with a crime. It's not my job, nor anyone else's here to decide on his guilt or innocence so I don't want to find anyone bullying him okay? Yes I know I lost my rag with him earlier and I've apologised to him for that and I intend to add that fact to my official report so everything is above board. I do have a code and when I'm wrong I'm big enough to admit it. Now I've told him that he can stay with us in here so he has access to food and drink; he's a person not an animal and I like to do things right. I'm asking for volunteers to sit with him on his table. Say, teams of four in two hour rotations? It's gonna have to be twenty four seven I'm afraid but all you have to do is make sure he doesn't run off, get him food and drinks and escort him to the bathroom and back. Okay so who wants to be on the first watch?"

Once Nembier had his first team with him, I got myself something to eat and sat down. By the time we all decided it was time to get some sleep, I'd got to know several of the inmates and found them to be nice guys. One of them, a middle aged man with a quiet way about him named Baz, turned out to be from Agrillia 3, so I took the opportunity to try to learn about the place. Nembier hadn't given me much of a clue except to ask me what I knew about the social history and laws, so I took a stab in the dark.

"What's life like on Agrillia Baz? Y'know, day to day."

"What's it like?" he asked. "Well umm, in what context? What's life like anywhere?"

"Well umm," I faltered as I tried desperately to think of what to say. "Is life easy for instance, or are there so many laws that you have to look over your shoulder all the time?"

"Well it's okay I guess," he said as he scratched his chin. "The authorities are pretty easy going most of the time. They let us get on with our lives without too much interference. It's more relaxed now than it was during the outbreak."

"The outbreak?" I asked. "What's that all about?"

"Well Sam, a couple of hundred years ago there was tragedy. A fusion reactor blew up and caused the atmosphere to become contaminated with a gas that made people sterile, so over time the population began to decrease rapidly as the elderly died off without there being a similar number of babies being born to keep the numbers steady. The scientists began to panic that we'd die out, so they sanctioned cloning as a way to get the numbers back up.

Everything was fine until the clones reached puberty and then many of them went crazy."

"Crazy? In what way crazy?"

"I don't know the finer details. I'm no scientist but it seems that once they hit puberty, the hormones somehow fucked with the wiring in their brains or something, because a large number of them turned into crazed killers."

"No shit?"

"No shit Sam," he nodded. "I remember hearing how thirty five percent of the first clone generation were guilty of murder. There was a whole wave of executions as the killings began. You see, once they sanctioned the cloning process, lots of couples went for it which resulted in many births happening around the same time and those babies all reached puberty around the same time. The killings all started around the same time too and in some cases, whole families were wiped out. I remember my grandfather telling me about a neighbour of his who came home and sliced up his wife and all four of his kids, then calmly made himself dinner and sat down and ate it without batting an eyelid. It was only when he hadn't reported for work for three days that someone went around to check, and they found him sitting in his garden as bold as brass while the bodies of his family stunk up the entire house."

"Damn, that's some weird shit," I replied, still trying to connect all the dots and understand how this affected Nembier and his case. "So what happened?"

"The authorities quickly passed laws outlawing any more cloning and they also passed a law preventing any clones from breeding, even the ones who hadn't gone crazy. All the ones who had killed were rounded up and executed and any children of clones were also rounded up and euthanased. The clones that remained and seemed healthy were sterilised and branded with a mark on the back of the neck but otherwise they were allowed to live reasonably normal lives, although they quickly found their neighbours weren't quite as friendly as they had been before."

"What an awful situation," I replied and he nodded.

"Yeah it was. It's referred to these days as the Agrillian outbreak. I'm surprised you didn't know about it."

"Well I've been around some, but I've never heard about it. Thanks for telling me though Baz, I'm extremely grateful to you. This information is very important."

"It is? How?" he asked.

"My prisoner is from Agrillia 3 and he is accused of nine murders. Murders he swears he didn't do. We had a teenage girl with us when we arrived here and she ended up with her throat cut not long after we arrived, at the same time as Nembier escaped from the restraints. I know she wasn't killed by the creatures and I feel sure that we're all meant to believe Nembier killed her, but something about it doesn't add up and I feel pretty sure he didn't do it."

"So what does that have to do with the outbreak?" he asked.

"Nembier hinted to me that someone let him out of his restraints. Someone he said he's seen before." I looked at Baz as he digested this information.

"But he didn't say who?" he asked.

"No," I admitted. "He's being cryptic and I can't blame him really. When you're handcuffed and powerless to control your own destiny, I guess it's natural to want to play a power game with your captors."

This job had quickly become far more complicated than I was comfortable with. My job may be complicated at times but it is also quite simple, at least in theory. All I have to do is find my target, catch him and deliver him to the relevant authorities; quick, clean and simple and that's the way I like it. Bang, bang, bang and on to the next. This Nembier business had got right under my skin and try as I might, I just couldn't shake this feeling that I had to find out what was going on, even though it's not strictly my job. Maybe it was Jena Marks' death that caused it; maybe I felt she needed justice. Whatever, I was hooked and I couldn't let it go. As we drank I thought about what Nembier told me and turned it over in my mind, trying to make some sense of it but the more I focussed on it, the fuzzier everything became. Someone had picked the locking mechanism of his restraints and let him out; someone he'd seen before. Those were the alleged facts but where the fuck was I to find the answers? What I needed to know was who had freed him and why? Nembier wasn't telling so I was on my own and as I ran a hand through my hair, I sighed with frustration.

"What's up Sam?" Baz's question brought me out of my musings.

"How the fuck am I going to find out who freed him and why?" I replied but he shrugged.

"Well what do we know?" he asked. "He said he's seen the person before." I nodded. "So we can assume that this encounter happened on Agrillia can't we?"

"Can we?" I replied with a shrug. "The guy is a scientist. He may have travelled all over the galaxy doing his thing."

"Exactly what is his thing?"

"Umm ancient Agrillian languages I think."

"But that's not something that's going to be of interest to many folks outside of Agrillia," he said. "Is it?" A light went on inside my mind at this comment and I had one of those moments of sudden illumination when things fall into place and form the beginnings of a pattern that I can recognise.

"You're right Baz. Ancient Agrillian languages might be very interesting to modern day Agrillians, but who else would be that interested huh? There may be other scientists from other worlds who would be interested in that sort of thing, but they'd travel to Agrillia to study it."

"Right," Baz grinned. "I'll bet you a clean fifty, the guy we're after is Agrillian, or at least that's where Nembier knows him from."

"The guy we're after?" I asked.

"Well, I'm happy to help," he blushed. "You've got me interested now Sam; you can't leave me out of it. I wanna play too."

It was fully dark as Baz and I traded ideas and since we all now knew the building was pretty secure, we felt it wasn't really necessary to have armed guards on watch while we slept. After arranging a change of teams to make sure Nembier was watched throughout the night I decided to get some sleep. Dex, Luggs, Baz and I decided to share one of the ground floor offices for the night and after a quick rearranging of desks to partition the room into sections, we tried to get comfortable. It was as I was trying to go to sleep that something occurred to me.

"Dex, Luggs are you awake guys?" I whispered.

"What's up Sam?" Dex replied.

"Can you remember how many passengers boarded the Sally B when you stopped at Agrillia?"

"Umm, I know quite a number disembarked there. I'd got talking to a couple of guys on the trip and they both got off there. One of them left the vidicom game he'd lent me, so I caught up with him at the disembarkation gate to give it back and there was a good hundred or so waiting to get off. I've no idea who got on there though, sorry buddy."

"Okay no worries."

"Sorry, I don't know either, "Luggs hissed, "but Morry might do. That's the sort of shit he deals with all the time. Ask him in the morning."

"Morry?" I frowned.

"Yeah, Morry Laymon. Our esteemed leader," he sniggered.

"Oh you mean Flark," I said without thinking.

"Flark?" Luggs asked. "Why do you call him that?"

"Oh he just looks like a Flark to me I guess."

"What's a Flark?" Baz asked.

"Back home on Sigma Prime, those who are wealthy enough can employ an android servant to help them around the home. They keep the house, cook and clean and stuff like that and they're all programmed to have this real simpering manner. It's all yes sir, no madam, have a wonderful day and would you like me to kiss your ass? Anyway, they're called Flarks and he reminded me of them when I first came aboard the Sally B." All three guys laughed till tears streamed down their faces and I knew that within twenty four hours of being back aboard the liner, the guy would be Flark to the whole crew. I hoped it didn't get back to him, at least not until I left on my next job.

It seemed as though I'd just got to sleep when I was woken up by someone shaking my shoulder and shouting my name. Dawn was just breaking as I opened my eyes to see Dex, stripped to the waist and eyes wide with shock shaking me awake.

"Sam, wake up buddy for fucks' sake wake up."

"What the fuck?" I groaned as I tried to come to my senses. The naked, leggy blonde faded into the mists as reality overtook me. "What's the problem?"

"One of the prisoners is dead."

"What?" I was awake at once and sat up and stared at him. "Who, how, what happened?"

"One of the prisoners from cell wing four we let out yesterday. He's dead, throat cut just like Jena Marks. He's in the bathroom."

"Oh shit," I cursed and got to my feet and dressed hurriedly.

"That's not all Sam," Dex said as I fumbled with the buttons on my shirt.

"Oh fuck, what else?"

"It was Nembier who found his body. The guys watching him took him to the bathroom to take a piss. They waited outside for him and he went in alone. They heard him yelling and went in to find the body, with Nembier standing over him."

It seemed that whenever I thought this crazy situation couldn't get any worse, it suddenly did and I found myself considering the wisdom of doing the job I do. Luckily I don't get this type of situation that often; most of the time it's a straight forward chase, catch and deliver but every so often a job comes up that makes me feel old and tired and this was one of those. It was one of those jobs when I wondered whether the money was really worth the hassle. I know I'm law enforcement and everyone thinks of us as low life's, Mercs, but some of us do have some kind of code we operate by and although I like a certain standard of living, I'm not a gold digger without principles. I do this job because it's what I know how to do and I do it well. I like the freedom it gives me and anyway, I'm too old to retrain but there are one or two of my jobs I would turn down flat if I could know in advance what was to transpire. This was already just such a job.

Dex led the way to the bathroom and I went in. A pair of feet stuck out from the stall at the far end. The body lay on its front with the head over the toilet, making it look like he was interrupted while taking a quiet puke after a heavy night of booze. I jotted down the number written on the collar of the prisoner's overalls he wore, before turning him over and lying him down. He had obviously been killed while taking a piss as his dick was still hanging out of his overalls. It's not my job to protect a victim's modesty but hey, I'm a guy too and I'd hate to think my corpse was laid out, dick exposed for all to see so I shoved it back inside and zipped him up. His throat had been sliced clean through to the spine and his head canted back far too far as I laid him down. Over the years I've been doing this job I've learned to have a strong stomach and I swallowed hard as I looked at the gaping slash and the mess it had made in the stall. Examining the wound, I could see his spine clearly, which told me both his carotid artery and jugular vein had been sliced through. Jeez no wonder there was so much mess in here!

I stood and looked at the wall above the toilet. His carotid artery had spurted blood with such a force that it hit the end wall and splashed in all directions. The walls and ceiling were covered and the floor was awash. Five or six spurts, a pint at a time hitting the end wall and splashing back in all directions would have ensured the killer was drenched in blood himself. A quick look around discovered no helpfully discarded weapon, so I went outside to ask questions. Nembier had found him, according to what Dex told me, so he was my obvious first port of call. He was in the canteen, still watched over by the same team who had escorted him to the bathroom. His face was grey and I noticed his hand shook as he lifted his drink to his lips. Sighing, I sat down and looked at him.

"So who wants to start?" I asked and looked at each face in turn. As the guys in his watch team went over what happened, I realised pretty quickly that Nembier couldn't have done it. They'd taken him to the bathroom and waited outside for him. They all agreed that it was less than thirty seconds before they heard him yell and went in to see what the fuss was about, to find him standing over the body with his hand over his mouth. He'd run into the adjoining stall to vomit and they all reckoned he didn't have the time to do it and I agreed; it would take longer than thirty seconds to slit someone's throat, wash and dry yourself and put clean overalls on, before screaming your lungs out and vomiting on cue. He couldn't have done it and I now had two options. Either the killer wanted to frame Nembier and was shit at it, or it was just pure coincidence that he was the next to want a piss after the guy met his end. Whoever did it would have been covered in blood and would need to wash and change his clothes and as I could see no one around who was in such a mess, I realised that somewhere in the building was a pair of bloody overalls. If I could find them I might get a DNA sample from them and maybe catch another killer and get a bonus on my pay check.

Nembier was worried that everyone would think he did it and worried for his safety and I have to admit that the same thought occurred to me too. My job was to deliver him, alive preferably and although I have the authority to use deadly force if absolutely necessary, my payout goes down if I deliver a dead cargo when my job was for a live one. I felt it pertinent to make an announcement; not just to protect Nembier and my pay check, but to prevent anyone else from committing a crime they'd have to pay for.

"Hey guys," I called and the room felt silent. "I just want you all to be aware that my prisoner here did not commit this crime. It was just coincidence that he found the body and maybe whoever did it wants us to believe he's guilty but I can assure you that he's innocent, of this crime at least. I hope everyone is clear about that okay?" I gave everyone as serious a glare as I could muster and heard a few sighs and saw a couple of nods in response. "Now, do we know who the victim is?"

"He was my cell buddy," a voice from my left called. A guy to my left, red eyed from crying was holding his hand up. "His name is Jallon Tyle and he's from Agrillia 3." This news stunned me and I shot a look at Nembier, who looked back at me with raised eyebrows. Agrillia 3 centre stage again. What is the significance of this? Nembier is from there and is connected to nine murders there. He was freed from his restraints by someone he said he met there; thereby implying they are Agrillian too. Now this latest victim is also Agrillian. I could see the pattern but couldn't explain it and it irritated the heck out of me. Something else then occurred to me and I looked for Flark.

"Captain?" I called, just managing to stop myself from calling him by his nickname out loud. "Do you know where Jena Marks was from?"

"Agrillia 3 Sam," he replied.

Now more than ever, I knew it was important that I find those discarded overalls so I asked for some volunteers to do a search. Around a hundred or so of the newly released prisoners from cell wing four stood up, so I split them up into groups of half a dozen and gave them each a territory to search.

"If you find them, don't touch them," I reminded them all. "Leave at least three guys watching them, the rest come and find me okay?"

CHAPTER SIX

Having so many volunteers to search for the discarded overalls meant I was able to give each group a fairly small territory. It also meant they could search that territory with great care. I told them to rip the place apart if necessary; those overalls must be found. They'd be found eventually, I knew that but I expected it to take at least a couple of hours before I got the call and I was more than a little surprised therefore, when one of the inmates came puffing into the canteen within thirty minutes and announced they'd found them stuffed inside an air conditioning vent. Whoever put them there was in a hurry and hadn't taken enough care to ensure the grating was put back properly and the loose screw and freshly scratched paintwork caught their attention.

"Well done guys," I grinned, inspecting the vent and its contents. "Great job." I sent one of them to fetch a bucket of water, some of the cleaning fluid we'd used the day before and a bin liner. When he returned I thoroughly washed the floor around the base of the vent. Then I squirted my hands with sterifilm and reached in to retrieve the overalls. They were a mess and the smell of blood filled our nostrils as I laid them on the newly cleaned floor to examine them. Blood soaked them from mid chest to the knees so I took several blood samples from different areas, confident that they would all be from the victim. Now I just needed to get a DNA sample of whoever had worn them and I'd have my killer. Experience told me my best hope was a hair or blood, but either of those could be from the victim. No, with so much blood and quite a few hairs already on them, I opted for sweat. Whoever wore them would naturally have sweated, so I took several samples from both armpits, the back of the neck and the crotch. I took some vidicom footage of them and put them into the bin liner. Once they were bagged and tagged, we all returned to the canteen for a drink.

As I sat and had a drink, I realised two things. The most important being that I needed to get the killer's DNA sample worked up. Ideally this would identify him immediately if he was in the law enforcement record system already but if not, at least it would identify his race, which would give me a place to start. Then I realised that my own equipment would not be able to do the job. I'm not a detective; I'm given a specific target to pursue and restrain and my equipment enables me to ensure I have the correct target; it doesn't enable me to work out who the target might be. For that I needed a lab; a lab with a sample processor. A voice brought me out of my musings and I looked up to find Clavan looking at me.

"What's up Sam?" he asked. "I'd have thought you'd be delighted now you've found the overalls and got your samples. Doesn't this mean you now know who our mystery slasher is?"

"Well no I'm afraid it doesn't," I admitted sadly. "I don't have the necessary equipment to run the DNA sample. All I can do is record it; I can't process it. I'd need access to a proper forensic lab with a sample processor."

"So why the long face?" he grinned. My frown made him snigger. "This is Floxham Island remember? Y'know, hub of the law enforcement universe?"

"Shit, of course it is." I almost yelled at my own stupidity. "Jeez how can I be so dense? There's bound to be a lab here. All I have to do is find it and hope it has power enough to work the sample processor. Thanks buddy."

"No problem," he grinned.

This knowledge brightened my spirits quite a bit and I leapt up and went over to where Flark was sitting, deep in conversation with a couple of the inmates. "Captain?" I asked. "Sorry to crash your rec time but where is that plan of the Island you had?"

"It's in the armoury. Is there a problem?"

"Not really," I replied, "but it might help me identify who killed Jenna and Mr Tyle."

"It will?" he frowned. "How?"

"I'm hoping there's a forensic lab here somewhere," I explained. "The samples I took from the overalls need to be processed before I can identify who they came from and my own equipment isn't able to do that. This being Floxham Island, I'm hopefully assuming that there'll be such a lab here somewhere. If there is and I can get over there and find it helpfully still with power, I can process those samples and at least partially identify our killer."

"Okay," he nodded as he stood up. "Come on then, let's take a look."

The forensic lab was easy to find on the plan of the island. Finding its location wasn't the reason I sighed heavily and swore. The reason for my mood was the fact that it was right on the other side of the island, at the furthest possible point from where we were all holed up, safe in the Admin Block. Flark sighed and ran a hand through his hair as he realised the full extent of our problem.

"Shit," I hissed. "It couldn't be any further away could it? Is nothing gonna go right for me on this job?"

"Dammit," he exclaimed and thumped the table. "Just when I was beginning to relax with the idea that all we had to do was stay inside here for another couple of days, this shit happens."

"I'm sorry buddy," I replied. I really did feel badly for the Liner's crew. They weren't paid to deal with situations like this and so far they'd all acted without reproach and I couldn't complain about any of them. If there was a way to get around having to involve them in any more danger, I'd take it happily.

"Don't apologise Sam," he sighed. "It's not your fault we have a maniac killer amongst us. What annoys me is that we've no choice but to get you out there to that lab. If we stay here and wait for rescue, more people could end up with their throats cut. But, if we make a run for the lab, we could all end up as dinner for those creatures. What a choice huh?"

"Yeah," I nodded. My mood was getting worse with each passing second but the guy was right and I couldn't argue his logic. "And you know what else is good? We could get there and find the lab without power anyway and our trip will have been a total waste of time." He turned away with his hand still grasping his hair and I made a snap decision that I knew was totally stupid and thankfully so did he. "Listen buddy, you and the crew aren't paid to deal with this shit. I'll go on my own and if I don't make it back, just promise me you'll get Nembier to the authorities and explain to them that there is substantial doubt as to his guilt okay?"

"What?" he yelled as he spun around and gazed at me wide eyed. "Are you crazy? That's the most ridiculous thing I've heard in years Sam," he said and started to laugh. Relief flooded through me and I could've kissed him. "And how the fuck do you expect me to deal with Luggs and Dex once they find out I've let you go out there alone huh?" he asked, eyes still wide with astonishment at my rash suggestion. "They'd skin me alive. Hell no Sam; even just for my own safety, you're not going out there on your own okay? End of discussion."

"Captain?" I asked with a grin.

"Yeah?"

"Give us a kiss," I laughed.

"Aww shucks Sam," he said as he burst out laughing.

Flark and I decided that it would be best not to let everyone know that I was going to be making a trip to the forensic lab to process the DNA sample I got from the discarded overalls. We agreed that to do so might alert the killer to the fact that he or she may soon be discovered and then either cover their tracks or go completely psycho in one last blaze of glory. Knowing that our best guns were going to be away from the group for a while and unable to give protection should that happen, made us both more than a little uneasy but there was no better option so we had to go with it. We knew that our disappearance would have to be explained somehow though, so I suggested we just tell everyone that we were going to scout around a bit to see if we could find some long range comms equipment we could use to alert the liner to come back for us. It seemed the logical thing to do and Flark agreed. We got back to the canteen and after taking Clavan into our confidence and gaining his promise not to spill the beans on the real reason for our trip, I took a deep breath and hoped I could lie convincingly.

"Okay listen up folks," I called and waited for the chatter to die down. "The Captain and I have decided that it would be sensible for us to try to get some help from somewhere rather than sit and wait for the liner to return. Now that another person has been killed it seems the logical thing to do. Now, we've looked at the plans of the island and we've located a couple of places we think give us the best opportunity of finding some long range comms equipment that will enable us to do that. The problem though, is that we're gonna have to work our way right across the island and you all know what's out there. Anyone who can handle a gun is welcome to volunteer but please, no sightseers this time okay? Be aware before you volunteer that you may not return. I'm sorry to be blunt but I can't sugar coat the dangers. Take twenty minutes to think about it and then we'll ask for volunteers." Before I'd even finished my speech, Luggs and Dex were at my side and within ten seconds of me finishing, Baz joined us. Cap appeared within another twenty seconds, shortly followed by half a dozen of the other inmates. With Flark and I, that made a dozen reliable guns and I was as happy as the situation allowed me to be. We felt we had the best chance possible of making it there and back without losing more than a couple.

Nembier looked at me with fear in his eyes so I decided to have a quiet word with him. "Hey guys, could you give us a minute?" I smiled at his watch team and they got up and left us alone.

He looked me right in the eyes and nodded slowly. "You're a decent liar Sam," he smiled, "but you can't fool me buddy. So what's really going on?"

"I got a DNA sample from the overalls the guys found and I need to process it before I can even have a chance of identifying the killer."

"So?"

"So I need a forensic lab with a sample processor to do that. My equipment won't do that job."

"Okay," Nembier nodded. "So why are you telling me?"

"Because if I don't make it back, I want you to know two things," I said as I held his gaze.

"And what would they be?"

"First, I know you didn't kill Jena Marks or Jallon Tyle. Second, I want you to know that I'm not totally convinced that you're guilty of the murders on Agrillia either."

His jaw dropped as he looked at me and tried to take in what he'd just heard. "You're not?"

"No, and I've asked the Captain to see to it that you get delivered to the relevant authorities if I don't make it back in one piece and to make sure they know there's some doubt as to your guilt. I'm telling you this so that you know I'm not some low life Merc who just sees guys like you as a pay check. I also hope that it helps you to understand the importance of allowing yourself to be delivered to the authorities without a fuss, so that the proper procedure and a full investigation can be undertaken. My official tag will ensure that my concerns are taken seriously, so don't think I'm handing you a bone to make you be a good boy okay?"

"I understand," he nodded and I noticed his eyes well up, "and thank you." I went to stand up but he put a hand on my arm. "Sam?"

"Yeah?"

"I mean it y'know. Thank you. Just in case you don't come back, would you allow me to shake your hand?"

The canteen was filled with voices and scraping chairs as I had a chat with the blue eyed plank who would be Acting Captain in Flark's absence and explained about changing Nembier's watch team every couple of hours. With a killer still on the loose I also told him to try to ensure no one went wandering around alone.

"Better try to keep folks in groups of three or four buddy," I suggested, "so that if the killer does strike again, we'll have some witnesses." He nodded. "Also, if the Captain and I don't make it back here, please get Nembier to the proper authorities and tell them I have substantial doubt as to his guilt. Here's my official tag number and the overalls we found are stowed away in the locked drawer in a desk in office number thirty seven, one floor above; the desk with the blue book on it. No one here knows I stowed them there okay, so don't let anyone know. We don't want them to go missing. Hand them over with Nembier and my tag number. Nembier won't give you any problems while I'm gone and he knows he has to be delivered to the authorities."

"Okay Sam." The blue eyes looked worried now. "No problem."

"I doubt we'll be back before nightfall," I added. "We're probably gonna have to hole up somewhere and make the trip back in the morning."

"Be safe and God speed." He offered me his hand, which I shook.

"Okay people," I called out and everyone looked up. "We're gonna be off now to the armoury and then we'll be on our way. We probably won't make it back here before dark so we'll be finding somewhere to hide until morning so don't worry if you don't see us back here before tomorrow. Now Chip here is gonna be Acting Captain in our absence, and although he only has official authority over the Liner crew and passengers, it would be a good idea for everyone to do as he asks. We really don't need any internal politics to add to our problems. Is everyone okay with that?" Nods and grunts filtered around the room so I nodded. "Okay guys, let's go."

The twelve of us made our way to the armoury to tool ourselves up. Once Flark and I explained the real reason for our trip, those of us already with weapons, loaded up on ammunition whilst the six inmates browsed the hardware on display. I watched them closely and was pleased when I saw them all choose powerful laser rifles. This told me they at least knew which weapon was appropriate for the job and weren't just tugging my chain when they'd volunteered. As I rooted amongst some crates I gave a little whoop of glee.

"Hey guys look at this," I exclaimed. "We have ourselves some Nozzies here."

"Great, gimme one them bad boys Sam," Dex grinned as he strode over, followed quickly by Luggs and the others. Nozzies are protective body armour vests that cover the entire upper torso, shoulders, upper arms, abdomen and groin areas. They're made of some sort of weird mix of a light metal and a volcanic rock from four of the Lymbin system's moons and their totally unpronounceable name begins with the word Noz something or other. They're standard kit in the military and law enforcement fields, and are known as Nozzies, for obvious reasons. They're extremely light and comfortable to wear but can withstand anything except the most powerful laser and pulse weapons. Oh, and they won't protect against the Hellfire Canon either but thankfully now that those Transmortals are gone, the Hellfire Canon will not be something we have to worry about encountering ever again and certainly not here on Floxham Island. We also hoped they would afford us protection from the teeth of any of those creatures outside that we might be unfortunate enough to get too close to. One of the inmates was rooting around in the cupboards and suddenly gave a yell that sent us all running over to have a look.

"Fuck me, look at that Sam," Luggs exclaimed with a grin.

"My god, I want one of those," Dex said and took another down for himself.

What we'd stumbled upon was a stash of fairly antique but pristine Incendipulse guns, together with hundreds of fuel canisters. These weapons send out a quick but deadly pulse of volatile energy that immediately bursts into flame as soon as it makes contact with anything. Very few things can withstand them, apart from solid rock, water or thick metallics. They're not just flame guns, they are portable mini volcanoes and I was delighted to see them.

"Shit," I hissed with awe as I handled one. "What a weapon this is. Has anyone here ever handled one in use?"

"Once," Dex nodded. "We had one in my military unit and I persuaded my captain to let me have a go one day."

"What are they like?" one of the inmates asked.

"Wow, they are damn awesome," Dex laughed and shook his head. "You have no idea."

"Okay let's have at least three of them with us okay guys?" I said and several bodies all rushed to grab one. "Okay, now if no one needs a piss or anything, let's get to it shall we?"

We grouped at the main entrance door and readied ourselves.

"Okay guys let's get the introductions over so we're all acquainted huh?" I smiled and they nodded. "I'm Sam as you already know so each one introduce yourself so we all know who we are."

"Morry Laymon, hi."

"Sergeant Dex Simmia. Dex for short. Hey guys"

"I'm Luggs."

"Bazlon Janks. Baz for short. Hi"

"Jo Capillianos. Cap for short."

"Hank Grollien. Hi."

"Rum Grelly but everyone calls me Grelly."

"Asken Stichings. Stitch for short."

"Tearlan Budjon. Bud for short."

"Carl Graskin."

"Stefano Masboyenkiaskonos. Boy for short."

"Great to meet you guys," I grinned. "Okay let's do this."

We exchanged glances and I nodded at Dex, who yanked the door open. We all leapt out, guns at the ready and squinted in the bright sunshine. Nothing leapt at us so after making sure the door was firmly closed behind us, we took a breath and regrouped.

"Okay guys," I hissed. "We won't have the flying things to worry about, they're night workers but we will have all manner of others. Just one thing by the way; those hunch backed things have shit eyesight so if they corner you, keep still and shut up. They work off sound and possibly smell too so if you keep quiet and don't fart, they won't know you're there. Just wait until they go away and save ammo. If anyone wants to back out, now's your last chance."

"We need eyes on each side and at the rear too," Dex ordered. "Come on guys, make a formation huh?" The plan of the island showed the lab to be right on the opposite side of the roughly circular area on which the facility was built, so we knew where we were going. We turned to our left and set off to make our way around to the rear of the Admin Block, trying not to look at the corpses that littered the ground. In this hot sunshine they were getting extremely smelly and a couple of the guys coughed as they breathed in. Some of them were ones we removed in our hastily arranged clean up operation, but many lay were they'd died. Not a single one was intact and there were many single limbs and a couple of heads lying about. This was the most horrific sight I had ever seen and I knew I'd be having some sleepless nights over it. As we followed the path around the gentle curve we saw a long low building, separated into five different sections come into view to our right.

"That's the main storage facility and shopping sector," Luggs hissed. "Right next to it is the shuttle landing pad. If we get short of anything, that's where ya go guys." It wasn't until we got further around to the rear of the cell wings that we noticed the huge rent in the storage facility roof. A large flap of the metal roofing material curved up and back and several broken pieces lay on the ground. Several of the shop doors were smashed off their hinges and boxes and cans lay strewn about as litter fluttered around in the gentle breeze.

"Well it's no surprise that the stores are gonna be a target huh?" Carl hissed. "Guess I'll be making do with nutri vend after all." Luggs snorted and grinned as he nodded in response.

"Keep that building in your sights at all times guys," Dex ordered. "With all that food stored inside there could be any number of creatures in there at any time of day or night okay?" We continued around to the rear of the cell wings and soon found ourselves looking at a large square building; the sign that hung limply from the post at the crossroad of three paths telling us this was the recreation centre. Every window was smashed through and the double doors stood open, propped there by a couple of chairs. It was surrounded on all sides by large gardens in which trees swayed gracefully in the gentle breeze. Short blue grass grew everywhere, lush from the generous rainfall and the tender care of the island's gardeners. Shrubs and bushes afforded us a little cover as we made our way forwards and we all noticed one of them had bright red flowers that smelled divine. A large pond flanked the right hand side of the Recreation Centre building with seats placed here and there around its edge.

"Keep that building to our left guys," Flark said. "It's the most direct route to the lab which should be directly behind it." There was just time to think that his last comment was probably tempting fate when we heard a loud roar from somewhere out of sight up ahead.

"Shit," Luggs hissed as he readied his laser rifle and snapped his head from side to side. "Where the fuck is that coming from?" The roar came again, definitely from somewhere up ahead.

"It's in front guys," I said as Flark and Dex both nodded. "Somewhere up ahead." Ahead of us was the corner of the recreation centre building. We ran to it and hugged the wall, thankful that there were no windows on this side through which something with large teeth could grab at us.

"It must be around the corner up ahead," Flark said, nodding towards where the wall we were all hugging, ended a hundred yards or so ahead of us. Before I could reply the roar came again, accompanied this time by three similar roars.

"Oh shit," I sighed aloud. "It's got friends."

"Well we have two choices," Baz whispered. "We either wait it out here and make them come to us, or we work our way to that corner and see what happens." I didn't like either of those choices and judging by the lack of response from the others, neither did they.

"Maybe they're not roaring at us," Grelly offered with a shrug. "Maybe it's just saying hi to its pals. Maybe they're fighting between themselves. Maybe they're fucking. We won't know if we stand here scratching our balls. We gotta move guys." Even though we were all scared out of our wits, we all knew he was talking sense. We couldn't just stand here; we needed to get beyond that corner to reach the lab anyway. We had no choice but to move.

"For fuck's sake I'm sick and tired of all this shit," Luggs said as he stepped away from the wall and strode along the path towards the corner with what was either the most hideously reckless abandon, or extreme bravery. Dex shouldered his rifle and stepped after him, followed by Baz, myself, Flark and then the six other inmates. We stepped out from the relative safety of the wall and took in the scene. In the large open parkland surrounded by the recreation centre behind us, the hospital and forensic lab ahead, the accommodation sector to the far left and the antenna and workshops to our right, a standoff was taking place. Two groups of creatures circled the prize that lay between them. Several corpses lay in a heap, steaming and rotting in the hot sun; the stench bringing tears to our eyes. One group were hairless, fat bodied things that walked on all fours; each of their slightly too long legs sporting one hoof and one vicious claw. At a rough guess they were about the size of a grown man, although their fat bloated bodies looked way out of proportion to the rest of them. A wide, blocky head sat atop a short but fat neck; the long, narrow jaws opening wide to reveal short curved teeth designed for ripping and tearing. Each had a long, hairless whippy tail at the other end that thrashed constantly. These were the source of the roars we could hear and we all reckoned they would carry for miles on the air. Those roars were aimed at the other group that faced them in this standoff and as I looked at them, I gasped in shock and looked at Dex who stood next to me, equally amazed.

The three of them stood roughly eight feet high, bipedal and covered with long sandy brown hair from head to toe with a darker stripe running down the back from the top of the head to the base of the spine. Their heads were slightly pointy on top and I could see very pronounced brow ridges that made me momentarily think of Luggs. I shook the thought away as I watched them facing the fat, bloated, roaring things; silent and staring despite the cacophonous roaring.

"My god they're humanoid," Baz remarked behind me and I just nodded in shock. Suddenly, one of the fat, bloated things leapt across the no man's land between the two groups towards the hairy humanoids who still stood silently waiting. The middle one then stepped forward and caught the creature in mid air and, grabbing one of its front legs in each hand, ripped its front legs clean off and dropped the rest to the floor where it lay screeching in its death throes. Two of the remaining fat creatures lunged forward as one towards the three upright sentinels as the remaining one lost its nerve and turned on its heels and ran off across the park towards the accommodation sector. Within thirty seconds all was quiet; the roaring creatures pulled limb from limb by the three strange humanoids who still hadn't uttered a sound. As they turned to leave, the smallest of the three suddenly turned and looked right at us; holding our gaze for long moments before rejoining his fellows and disappearing behind the other side of the recreation centre building. What I saw in those few moments will stay with me for the rest of my life and will, no doubt, haunt my dreams from time to time. What I saw was not wild survival driven by instinctive, animalistic urges. What I saw was intelligence, understanding and comprehension. What I saw was myself looking back at me. I was so shocked I couldn't speak or move and it wasn't until I felt someone shaking my shoulder that I shook my head and came to.

"Did you see that?" I whispered. "Did you see what I saw?"

"Yeah, I saw it Sam," Dex replied, his eyes wide and as unbelieving as mine must've been. "I saw it but I don't believe it."

"It knew," a small voice behind me said and I turned to find Boy with tears in his eyes staring back at me. "It knows," he repeated and we all understood and nodded. "It knows what it is. It has understanding of itself. They're just like us."

"It's gonna take me a long time to get my head around this shit," I said as I ran my fingers through my hair, "and I may never achieve that but one thing I do know is that they never tried to kill us or harm us, so I say we avoid killing them unless they directly attack us okay?" Everyone nodded immediately.

"It would be like killing another person in cold blood," Luggs remarked. "I couldn't do that, not after it looked at me that way. Shit that's gonna give me goose bumps for months."

"Okay guys let's go," I said. "The lab is just across the park, at the right hand side of the hospital. The sooner we get there and check the place out and make it safe, the better." We set off towards the lab, the wide open space all around us making us all nervous and jumpy. Halfway across a voice from my right made us all stop dead in our tracks.

"Hey guys, we've got company at three o clock." My heart fell as I snapped my head around and saw the huge lumbering hunch backed thing stomping towards us.

"Okay now quiet guys," I hissed. "Those guys are blind in daylight but they can hear a butterfly farting three miles away so stand still and shut up until it's gone, and no farting either just in case it has a great sense of smell too." The smell of the pile of corpses must be quite a draw and I suddenly wished we weren't so close to the source of that smell. It stomped towards us, head bobbing from side to side so its ears and nose could guide it towards the heap. As the seconds ticked by agonisingly slowly, it passed within a few feet of us and I'll go to my grave swearing on oath that not one of us dared to breathe for several minutes. The ground shook as it stomped past us and I slowly brought my head around and followed it with my eyes as it headed right for the pile. Still not daring to move, I watched as it circled, sniffing its way to the tastiest morsel.

"When I say, we move silently towards the lab. Okay guys?" I whispered. "Wait for my word or we're all dead." As patiently as I could, I watched the creature as it continued to circle the pile and then lady luck smiled upon us. With its back to us, it dropped its head and began to eat. "Now," I hissed. Together, the twelve of us ran on tip toes towards the lab building up ahead and even through the seriousness of the situation, the sight of Dex, a large black man with a military bearing tip toeing along like a ballet dancer, carrying a laser rifle in one hand and an Incendipulse gun in the other, was so hilarious I had to force myself to look away for fear of bursting out laughing.

Right umm, I'm gonna sign off now. I'm tired and need to take a shower and hit the sack. I'll pick you all up again in the morning after breakfast. This is V-log reference AZ267/M, data log reference point 2458712/6543. Good night all.

CHAPTER SEVEN

Morning folks. This is V-log reference AZ267/M, continuing report. Data log reference point 2458712/6544.

Now where was I? Oh yeah, the lab. Y'know, those hairy humanoid things really shocked the wind out of me. I guess everyone knows a little about evolution but we're all used to being what we are today, right now and I suppose it's natural for us to believe we're the only truly sentient beings out there. It's not until you're faced with something like those things we saw that you realise how far we've come and y'know, there was just something completely unsettling about looking into those eyes and seeing what we saw looking back at us. The fact that it looked basically humanoid didn't bother me so much, or any of the other guys but the understanding in those eyes, the awareness, that's what did it. It was as if, in that moment when it locked eyes with us, it spoke to us about ourselves and unless I'm going completely crazy I swear I saw disappointment in those eyes. In fact, Baz told me later that he reckoned it looked at us accusingly, as if it was asking us what the fuck we were doing and where we thought we'd gone wrong. Several minutes later I realised it was shame that looked back from those eyes. Not the self critical shame of someone who knows he's said something offensive and feels bad but too embarrassed to apologise but the sort of shame when you look at someone and realise you're not that proud to be the same race or species.

Anyway, we ran as silently as we could on tip toes across to the lab and made for the far wall so the building would be between us and the dinner party going on behind us. The main entrance was halfway down this end wall, flanked by windows on either side.

"We're nearly there guys," I hissed as I got my breath back. "Let's check through these windows before we make for the door though. We don't want to go bursting in there until we know what may be hiding or sleeping in there." Dex was at the front of our group so he edged forward and peered in the first window, cupping a hand to block out the light.

"There's a small room inside this window," he whispered. "Looks like there's refrigerators full of bottles and test tubes. There's a table in the middle and a couple of chairs knocked over. There's a door standing open that looks like it leads towards the main entrance, maybe a reception area or something. It looks safe to me; can't see anything lurking there."

"Okay, onto the next window," I nodded and we crept forward towards the main entrance door which was flanked by floor to ceiling glass panels either side. Dex leaned forward and peered in, but immediately snapped his head back so fast he banged it against the wall and winced.

"There's a crowd of those things in there," he hissed. "Those things we saw back there," he nodded back towards where we'd encountered the hairy humanoids.

"Those hairy people?" Bud whispered from behind me

Dex shook his head. "No, the other ones, the bald ones the hairy people killed. There must be at least half a dozen in there."

"Okay," Flark hissed from a little further back down the line. "We have enough fire power to deal with them easily enough, don't we?"

"Yeah, they'll be no problem," I nodded, "but we need to know what else is in there so we can be prepared huh? Maybe we should scout the other windows too?"

"But two of those windows are back around we're we've just come from," Cap said. "That would mean we'd have to go back out into the open and risk bumping into the hunch back." Several of the guys were shaking their heads in horror at my suggestion.

"He's right Sam," Luggs said. "We're gonna have to just go in and keep firing until nothing else moves. Then we barricade ourselves in before the noise attracts everything else in the vicinity." This wasn't the ideal solution either but I had to admit that it was the only sensible plan available to us at the time. We couldn't risk getting near the hunchback again and I reckoned its dinner was going to last a while. We had no choice but to go in blind.

"Shit," I exclaimed. "I hate not having the upper hand. Okay, what do we have that makes the least noise?"

"I'd say the Incendipulse is the quietest we have but they're messy. We could set the whole building on fire." Luggs said and Dex nodded. "The laser rifles make more noise but they're quick, more controllable and less messy."

"Yeah, let's go with the rifles," Flark remarked and both Dex and Baz nodded.

"Okay," I replied. "Three guys with the Incendipulse guns keep to the rear and cover our asses. It looks to me like three of us will fit through that door at a time, so here's what we'll do. Three go in and drop to your knees. Three more go in and hunker down low and the last three go in standing up. That way we don't run the risk of shooting each other. Any questions? Okay who's up first?"

Dex and Luggs handed their incendipulse guns over to Boy and Carl and stepped forward with Flark. Baz, Cap and Grelly stood behind them. Myself, Stitch and Bud came up next, leaving Boy, Carl and Hank with the Incendipulse guns at the rear.

"Okay guys," I whispered, "you ready?"

"Hell yeah," Luggs grunted. "Let's get those bastards."

"Okay then, remember what to do," I reminded them. "Dex, Luggs, Morry, you guys drop right to the floor okay? You don't want your heads blown off now do ya? Baz, Cap and Grelly, you drop down into a crouch so me and umm."

"Stitch."

"And I'm Bud."

"Right," I replied. "So Baz, Cap and Grelly, you guys hunker down a bit so Stitch, Bud and me don't give you an unexpected haircut. Right, let's go."

The main door to the lab was open a crack and Luggs gave one almighty kick and we lunged in as one. The three guys in the front row dropped onto their asses, the next three dropped to their knees and us three in the third row stepped forward behind them as we all began firing together. The inside of the small reception area exploded as our laser rifles found their targets. All seven of the bald creatures were killed within fifteen seconds before they'd had time to register what was happening. We stopped firing and the sudden silence was deafening after the racket our rifles had made and I could hear the blood pumping in my ears. We just had time to take a breath before we heard what was now a familiar screech.

"Oh no," Luggs sighed.

"Shit and fuck," Dex hissed.

We were in a small square reception area. Two doors led off to our right, another two on our left and ahead of us, a short corridor led to another door. Both doors on our right stood open and one of those to our left. The screech came again followed by another and we all knew what was coming. Out of the corner of my eye I saw shadows through one of the doors on our right.

"To the right guys, they're in there." The nearest door on our right suddenly burst off its hinges and the creature struggled to get through the gap; its huge leathery wings getting in its own way and giving us valuable seconds. We opened fire and its head burst open, spraying blood over its companion who was also struggling to get through the narrow doorway. We kept firing and it dropped to the floor on top of its headless companion. A crash from the adjacent office caught our ears and we looked toward the open door. Another crash and a thump followed in quick succession and then it stepped into view.

The humanoid must've been nearly eight feet tall and stood looking at us. Clearly a male, his long brown hair smelled strongly of unwashed armpits and sweaty crotches and I noticed his eyes were pale grey. His nostrils twitched as he sniffed the air, as if he was trying to figure out what we were. We were mesmerised into silence as we stood there, looking at him looking at us. I was about to speak when the smallest of shadows right behind him caught my attention. I shifted my gaze to his left and saw the large blocky head and gaping jaws of another fat bloated creature creeping out from over the pile of dead flying things. It must've smelled the hairy guy, as it turned towards him and growled menacingly. Without thinking I opened fire and blood gushed from an artery in its neck as it fell to the floor behind the hairy guy, who spun around in shock and looked at the creature lying dead at his feet.

"Guys," I whispered as calmly as I could. "Move away from the door so he can leave; I don't feel comfortable shooting him." My companions nodded and I heard Luggs grunt in agreement as we all shuffled out of the way, leaving a clear route to the main door. The hairy guy continued sniffing the air and kept looking towards the door; his eyes flitting from the door to us and back again. Once, when he looked right at me, I did something so instinctive and natural that it wasn't until afterwards that I realised how significant it was. He looked right at me and I nodded towards the door and then smiled at him. It seemed so natural that I almost spoke to him but managed to stop myself just in time. He let out a snort and took a tentative step towards the door, his eyes on us all the time. We shuffled back as far as we could and the hairy guy snorted again, before stomping towards the door and out into the sun. We ran shut the door behind him and sighed heavily.

"Come on," I encouraged, "we have to check out the other offices before we can relax and we should get these carcasses outside too." Twenty minutes later we sat in what we found to be a small kitchen and tried to calm ourselves. Talk was about the hairy guy and what a weird experience it was meeting him. Everyone agreed it made us very uncomfortable being near him. Not because he was dangerous because we all reckoned he wasn't. It was his unsettling sameness to ourselves while still effectively being a wild animal that freaked us out so much.

The fact that we were now enjoying a hot drink assured us that the lab did indeed have a working power supply as Dex confirmed when he discovered a solar generator in a small cubby hole. This was the first time I felt something had gone right for me and I sighed with relief and hoped that whatever happened during the next few hours, the solar cells on the roof of this building remain intact long enough for my DNA sample to be processed. Dragging myself to my feet, I got up and went into the main lab and examined the array of equipment and machinery within. Most of the stuff was unrecognisable to me but I'd watched samples being processed a few times so I knew what I was looking for and was confident I could work the machine. Thankfully I eventually found the sample processor at the far end of the room and switched it on and watched as lights flickered and a faint hum could be heard. Closing my eyes, I thought back to the last time I'd watched a sample being processed. It was a pretty straightforward procedure but I wanted to avoid any mistake so I went through it in my head a few times before I got out my mobile sampler and connected it to the docking plug on the top of the machine. A red light appeared on a panel at the front, which flickered a few times before turning to orange and eventually, to green. To say I was relieved would be putting it mildly and I sighed now that my device had been recognised and accepted by the machine and watched the digital screen as a display of my name, tag number and sample log numbers popped up. Then just a tap on the display screen to process the appropriate sample, wait for the beep and the whirring noise that would tell me the machine was working and I could relax. Once I was satisfied I went back to the kitchen and sat down with the guys.

"Everything okay Sam?" Flark asked and I nodded.

"Yeah. The sample is working up now. We just have to sit tight and wait for it to finish."

"How long will it take?" Luggs asked.

"Several hours I'm afraid," I shrugged. "It'll be dark before it's finished so we'd best resign ourselves to spending the night here."

"We'd better barricade ourselves in don't you think?" Stitch remarked and Dex nodded.

"Yeah, let's get all the desks out of the offices and pile them up against the main door." He stood but I raised a hand.

"There's loads of windows here though Dex," I said, "and those things could easily break in via any of the offices here. How about we barricade the main door as you said, but then we do the same in the main lab. There's no windows in there and there's lots of desks, tables and heavy machinery we can make use of."

"Yeah, good idea," Flark nodded. "We can take the nutri vend from here and anything we find in the cupboards too so our night can be relatively comfortable."

"It's a shame the laser net isn't working," Hank sighed and scratched his chin.

That's one thing we all agreed on and I nodded. If that thing was working it would be a breeze surviving here for the next few days. "Hell yeah," I agreed, "that would be wonderful. Once we killed everything we'd have no problems surviving here until the liner comes back."

"Well there's no point wasting time wishing for something you can't have," Luggs remarked as he stood and headed towards the door. "Come on then, let's get these desks moved."

"But that's just it," Hank continued. "It's not impossible." We all turned and looked at him questioningly. "I know I'm a prisoner here like all the other guys. I'm here because I stole money from the company I own, or rather the company I used to own."

"So?" Dex asked.

"So before I came here," he smiled. "Before I got found out that is, I had my own company that manufactured and installed security systems. Laser security systems to be exact." We all looked at him open mouthed. Dex, Flark and I looked at one another in amazement.

"You did?" Dex replied and Hank nodded.

"Yeah."

"So do you reckon you could get this one working again?" I asked.

"Well I don't know," he sighed. "You see, my company installed mainly small stuff. Y'know, residential and small companies. Nothing on this scale but the principle is the same. A laser is a laser. It's just how you use it that's different and the set up for a security system is basically the same whether you're installing at a small house or huge company headquarters. It's just the initial groundwork that's difficult; the logistics of working out the grid patterns needed to cover the area you want covered. Once that's been done it's just a case of wiring up the power supply and switching on."

"The island uses power from the planet's own magnetic field to power itself," I remarked and Hank nodded.

"Yeah I know and I wouldn't have a clue how to set that up."

"Shit," Flark exclaimed.

"But don't you see?" Hank said. "All the initial workup has already been done when the island was built. The only thing that's happened here is that it's gone wrong somehow. Maybe the antenna has broken or a wire has come loose, whatever, but the thing is it should just be a repair job not a full installation."

"If the antenna has broken, how can we fix it?" Boy asked.

"Well," Hank replied. "The antenna itself is just a metallic tube about ten feet high. The important bit is the laser generator at its tip and the magnetic field receiver at its base. The mag receiver collects power from the planet's magnetic field, as you already know. It sends that power up to the laser generator nipple that must be perfectly aligned with the receiver below in order for the power to flow around to the laser transmitters that will no doubt, encircle the entire island. If the tube itself is broken but the laser generator and mag receiver are intact, then we can just repair the tube or even stick a new post in the ground and re align the mag receiver with the generator nipple and it should automatically switch itself back on. In theory anyway."

"And how do we make sure it's aligned perfectly?" Cap asked, his engineering brain already working on the same wavelength as Hank's.

"There should be a sensor on the mag receiver that fits over the mouth of the power outlet. Another one sits over the generator nipple and the two of them will only link up and connect when they can both see each other perfectly."

"So how do we do that?" Luggs asked, his voice now slightly higher in pitch that signalled his rising annoyance.

"We look for the little blue lights," Hank smiled.

"Blue lights?" I remarked with a frown.

"Yeah," Hank nodded. "The sensors will light up blue when they're properly aligned and the power should begin to flow automatically around the whole laser network and the net will be back up to full working power within seconds."

"So you mean we just jiggle them around until we see blue?" Carl asked and Hank nodded.

"Well yeah."

"So what are we waiting for?" Bud grinned.

"Wait guys, wait," I said, holding up a hand as Luggs stood and headed towards the door. "Look outside."

"Huh?" Luggs remarked and I nodded towards the windows beside the main door.

"Look," I repeated. "It's already late afternoon. It will be dark here within a couple of hours and I really don't want to be outside there in the dark. We should wait until the morning and think about doing it then. We'll have the whole day on our side and none of those flying things to worry about."

"Aww c'mon Sam," Luggs grinned. "Don't go all limp on me now buddy."

"He's right," Hank said and Luggs's smile fell from his face. "It's a job that can't be done in a few minutes and remember this isn't really my bag. Although I know the principle of it I've never actually done something like that on this scale under these conditions. Even if everything goes perfectly to plan it'll take over an hour and then we have to get there, hope there's some tools, do the job while fighting off creatures and then get back."

"And remember as it gets darker and darker, there will be more and more creatures and they'll get bolder and bolder," Boy added.

"And there may be creatures we haven't met yet," Grelly remarked. "Worse ones."

Between the twelve of us we hefted all the desks we could find from the offices and piled them against the main door. By chance I found a couple of brooms in a cupboard and propped them under the handle and Luggs burst out laughing.

"Well Sam," he guffawed. "Thank god you found those brooms. For a minute there I thought we were mincemeat." The little reception area was filled with the sound of twelve men laughing their heads off and I had to admit, it was funny.

"You can laugh guys," I tutted at them with a grin, "but if these things prevent those things from getting inside here, you're gonna be awfully red faced in the morning."

"Yeah okay," Luggs replied between guffaws. "Come on then guys, let's get into the lab and secure the place huh?"

Baz and Hank shifted the nutri vend into the main lab while the rest of us began shifting tables and desks and everything heavy we could find. Grelly came running in with a bin liner full of snacks he'd discovered in one of the cupboards and an empty 5 gallon can that once contained something blue.

"What's the can for?" I asked.

"We're in here all night Sam," he grinned. "Maybe you can wait till the morning to take a piss but I sure as hell can't."

"Oh sure," I grinned. "Yeah, of course."

"Hey guys," Carl called out. "If anyone needs to take a shit, can you go do it now?" The lab was again filled with the sound of twelve guys laughing their heads off.

We spent a relatively quiet evening barricaded inside the lab. We passed the time by exchanging life stories and the guys got me to tell them of some of my more memorable adventures chasing the various criminals and crazies I deal with. The guys told jokes and we laughed till our sides ached and for the first time in ages I felt like one of the guys. It then occurred to me just how long it had been since I'd been able to just chill with some guys and have a laugh and I felt sad that it took such an awful situation to make it happen again. We agreed on a three hour watch rotation and half of us settled down to sleep on the cold floor of the lab. In my dreams I woke up and found myself alone except for hundreds of hairy humanoids all accusing me of wasting all those years of evolution and telling me how ashamed they were of what I'd done with my evolutionary advancement and when Flark shook me awake for my turn on watch, I felt worse than when I'd gone to sleep. I must've looked it too.

"You okay Sam?" he asked with a frown. "You don't look well buddy."

"Huh?" I yawned and rubbed my hands through my hair. "Oh yeah I'm fine thanks. Just a nightmare I guess. Anything exciting happen?"

"Nope," he said and shook his head. "Just a few growls and screeches in the distance and a couple of times we heard something thudding on the main door but I don't think they've broken through, yet. Must be those brooms of yours."

"Okay," I grinned as I got up and headed to the nutri vend for a hot drink. Several times during our three hour watch, we heard haunting howls from somewhere outside that creeped us all out and a couple of times we heard thumping from the main door. The last time we heard the thumping, it was followed shortly by what could only be the clatter of wood on a stone floor. Luggs burst out laughing so hard he spilled his drink and soon we were all in tears of laughter. Just as the end of our three hour watch was drawing close, we all heard the unmistakeable cry of something huge right outside the main door. The cry was accompanied by several loud thumps on the door and although I couldn't explain it, something about it made me stand up and head for the door of the lab.

"What the fuck is that?" Luggs said as the cry and the accompanying thumps came again.

"It sounds like something huge," Grelly added.

"I know this is gonna sound weird guys," I said, "but something about it makes me want to go and take a look."

"What?" cried Boy. "You're crazy."

"Maybe," I replied as the cry came again, "but it sounds like someone in pain don't you think? I wanna go take a look anyway, humour me huh? Now help me move all this junk will ya?" We managed to make enough room for me to squeeze through into the reception area and I crept towards the main door. Suddenly the door was thumped violently and the remaining broom fell to the floor but this time I didn't laugh. The cry came again and I was certain it sounded like someone in pain. There was just something desperate about it that got to me. Gingerly I peered through the glass at one side of the door and gasped in shock at the scene that greeted me. Outside the door was a huge male hairy guy thumping for all he was worth on the door. Beside him, on the ground lay a screaming and obviously heavily pregnant female. Movement caught my eye and I looked into the gloom behind them to see three hunchbacks lumbering towards them. My mind snapped into action and I didn't wait to debate with myself as to whether I was crazy or not, I just went into auto mode.

"Guys," I screamed. "Guys, get out here quickly and help me please. Guys, guys?" The six of us hastily moved the barricade enough for me to open the door and I reached for the handle.

Luggs put a hand on my shoulder. "Are you sure Sam?" he asked. His hesitation was understandable but I hesitated for no more than a second before yanking the door open and stood looking up at the hairy guy. Our eyes met and for a moment, time stood still. After just seconds the spell was broken and I beckoned to him to come in and stood back as he lifted the female to her feet and stomped into the building with us. We rearranged the barricade and I replaced the brooms before turning around and sighing. This was the first time I wondered what the fuck I'd done but it was too late now, they were in there with us and we had to hope my hunch was correct.

"Come on guys," I said as I led the way, "let's get back into the lab huh?" We moved towards the lab and I continued to beckon to the hairy guy. He looked at the lab door, then back to me, then down at his female who gave another loud cry, before lifting her up and following us. The commotion woke the sleeping guys, who all nearly fainted when they saw the hairy guy lumbering in behind us.

"It's okay guys, relax," I said, trying to sound confident. "He won't hurt us. His female is in labour, at least I think she is. Does anyone know how to deliver a baby?"

"I don't believe this is happening," Dex said rubbing a hand over his face and sitting on the floor.

"I once watched my sister give birth," Cap said. "She went into labour early and we couldn't get her to the medical facility in time, so her son ended up being born at home. It all seemed to happen naturally and she just yelled her head off and pushed." He shrugged. "Sorry, I'm not much help but that's how it was."

The hairy guy laid his mate down at the far corner of the room and was whimpering as she cried out and kept looking over at us. The way he looked at me told me that he wasn't just an anxious father. Something was wrong and he wanted us to help. What the hell I was supposed to do was beyond me so I leapt up and headed to the nearest digital console and tapped in *problems giving birth - humanoids'* and waited. A screen came up with a whole list of things that could cause problems, many of which I was able to dismiss right away. How long she'd been in labour was a mystery to me so I took a stab in the dark and opted for *baby stuck in birth canal - possible causes.'* I read a bit and then ran over to the female. This could be very awkward as I needed to see her most private parts and wasn't quite sure how the big guy would react. Taking a deep breath to calm myself, I looked at him and smiled and nodded slowly. He whimpered at me pleadingly so I took another deep breath and reached out to the female. As gently as I could, I spread her knees and looked at her crotch area. As she moaned in obvious agony, I could instantly see something trying to force its way out so I reached out and gingerly felt around with my fingers until I realised I was feeling a tiny bottom.

"Oh shit," I cried.

"What's up Sam?" Dex asked.

"It's coming out bottom first. What the fuck do I do?"

"That's gonna tear her apart," Baz replied.

"You'll have to push it back up," Luggs said. We all looked at him accusingly but he raised both hands. "I'm not joking Sam. Wait until she's between pains and then push it back a tiny bit and you'll free up the legs so they can drop down and come out first. Just a tiny bit mind, don't be forceful about it or you could do more damage. Then use your fingers to gently free up the legs so they can drop down."

"Aww hell I can't believe I'm doing this," I groaned and took another breath. When the pain seemed to finish I inserted my fingers again and gave a tiny push. Nothing happened so I pushed a little harder and felt my fingers go inside her a little further. "It's working I think," I cried. "I felt it move back up." This was encouraging so I gave another push and it moved some more.

"Get your other hand in if you can and feel around for the legs," someone called from behind me. Leaning forwards, I reached up with my free hand and was able to insert two fingers. For agonising seconds I rooted around and was just about to despair when I felt a thigh wriggle between my fingers. It felt wet and slippery as I scrabbled my fingers down over a tiny kneecap and then clasped the lower leg and wriggled it free. The guys gave a cheer as they saw the leg dangle from the female's crotch and I sighed and grinned.

"Now the other one Sam," Dex called. "Go on, you can do it buddy." The female's breath came in short gasps and I had to wait as another pain ravaged her and threatened to push the baby back down again. Once the pain dissipated I reached back in and easily found the other leg now that the first was out of the way. It was a much easier task to wriggle it down and both legs dangled free at last. The guys gave another cheer as I retrieved my other hand and sighed with relief. Suddenly the female gave another almighty push and a tiny hairy gal shot out into my lap. She was lifeless and I went cold. Suddenly Luggs was beside me and grabbed the little one and rubbed her back vigorously. Within a few seconds she began to cough and splutter and give a weird mewling noise. The guys all cried out in relief and I grinned from ear to ear. Sighing heavily and now sweating profusely, I gently laid her on the ground by the female's belly and we stepped away.

"Well done Sam," Dex said and clapped me on the back. "That was fantastic work buddy. Good work Luggs, how did you know what to do?"

"My grandfather had a farm and I used to help him when his animals gave birth. He always did that if any of them were lifeless at birth and it often brings them back. It encourages their breathing reflex or something."

"Awesome job you two," Baz grinned as all the guys congratulated us and I felt proud.

"Did that really happen?" I asked with a grin and began to laugh. Pretty soon the lab was once again filled with the sound of twelve guys laughing their heads off and in the far corner, a new life began amidst the violence and turmoil on Floxham Island.

CHAPTER EIGHT

To say that was a weird experience would be totally underestimating how it felt. I mean c'mon, how often does a guy get to deliver a baby to a huge, hairy humanoid throwback huh? It's not exactly on my job description and not something I would ever have expected to be doing but I think I handled it well considering the circumstances we were in. The guys and I got ourselves a drink from the nutri vend to wet the little gal's head and Luggs even came up with a name for her.

"You've found your new vocation Sam," Dex remarked.

"I don't want to be doing that again too soon," I laughed.

"Hey is it a boy or a girl?" Luggs asked.

"It's a girl."

"Then," Luggs began as he raised his right hand dramatically and placed his left on his chest, "by the power vested in me I hereby name this child Floxy." We all thought that was a great name so we drank a toast to welcome Floxy to the family. Hearing my name called, I turned and saw Baz sitting at a desk at the other end of the lab so I strolled over and saw he was reading something on a digital console.

"Found something interesting Baz?" I asked and he looked up at me and nodded.

"Yes actually I have. This is a journal kept by one of the scientists who worked here. A Doctor Sulleman his name is, I mean was. He talks about the hairy guys a lot."

"He does?"

"Yeah. Here, take a seat and listen to this."

It seemed that when Floxham Island prison was being built, they noticed the hairy guys hanging around nearby. They didn't seem scared by the invaders, nor did they show aggression and in fact there was a report of one of them saving the life of a workman who was attacked by one of the hunchbacked creatures. After that incident, the workmen started cultivating their friendship and pretty soon, they were acting as bodyguards for the men who were building the island. Once the building was finished and the workforce took up residence, they were allowed the run of the island in return for doing some basic manual labour from time to time.

After a couple of years the hairy guys started to die off rapidly and the island's scientists were baffled as to why. Not until there was just a handful left did they discover that the immigrant workforce had passed on their own pathogens to them, against which they had no immunity. The scientists immunised the remaining handful to save them from extinction and encouraged them onto the island as much as they could so they could be monitored more closely.

Over the years it became apparent that the hairy guy's gene pool was far too small and the offspring that survived birth were often deformed and died pretty soon after. Doctor Sulleman added fresh DNA to the hairy guy's gene pool by replacing some sections of their genetic code with fresh humanoid DNA. It should've worked but with the hairy guy's numbers already being so low, there wasn't enough time to perfect the process and raise the numbers. The last entry Doctor Sulleman made before the island crashed stated that in his opinion, the ones he had named Adam and Eve were the last mated pair of their kind along with another single male he had named Omega. The doctor built up quite a close relationship with them and tried his best to keep them healthy by administering to any of their medical needs and they came to trust him by coming to him when they felt they need his expertise. He delivered two offspring for Adam and Eve which were both stillborn and he feared they were never to become parents.

"Well Doc," I said aloud, "you have a new grand daughter now named Floxy and she's healthy and beautiful." Suddenly our attention was drawn to a noise in the far corner and we all turned and watched as the big hairy guy who I now knew was named Adam, held his newborn in his arms and crooned to her softly in eerily undulating tones that made the hairs on my arms stand up. We were transfixed and watched and listened in silence for many minutes, no one wishing to break the spell.

After several minutes I tiptoed back over to the guys and told them what Baz and I read from Doctor Sulleman's log entries. By the time I'd finished, Luggs was in tears and Dex teased him mercilessly.

"You're an old woman Luggs, you know that buddy?"

"You unfeeling bastard Dex," he countered and we all laughed till our sides ached.

It was morning so we decided it wouldn't hurt to go and see if it would be possible to get the laser net up and running again. We got ourselves ready and began shifting the barricade from the lab door. As we were about to leave I heard a noise behind me and turned to see the hairy guy Adam standing at the far corner with his newborn in his arms. He grunted at me softly, before looking down at the baby with what I can only describe as love. He then looked back up at me and grunted softly again. I was moved and struggled to contain my emotions.

"You're welcome big guy," I smiled. "She's beautiful. We'll be back in a little while okay? Just sit tight." All was silent as I turned back to find eleven faces staring at me with raised eyebrows and although I tried hard not to, I blushed to the roots of my hair. "What?" I demanded, trying to sound off hand but these guys weren't fooled and they all started to laugh.

We moved the barricade just enough to allow us to slip out so that the hairy guy could replace it if he needed to. We stole through to the reception area and checked the offices but found nothing sinister. We readied our laser rifles and I reached out and removed the brooms which were still firmly wedged against the main entrance door. There was no backing out now so I shot a look at Luggs and raised my eyebrows as I made a dramatic show of showing him each of the brooms and he was almost pissing his pants laughing.

"Everyone ready? I asked. Grunts and nods replied immediately so I opened the door a crack and peered outside into the bright sunlight. Two hunchbacks were sitting down a hundred yards away and resembled two elderly men passing the time of day.

"There are two hunchbacks a hundred yards away at two o clock," I said and Luggs, Dex and Baz stepped forward and nodded. We readied our rifles and I yanked open the door. The two hunchbacks were dead quickly and we formed a tight bunch while we checked all around three hundred and sixty degrees. All seemed quiet and I was just about to sigh with relief when Grelly called from the back of our circle.

"Okay we got company back here guys." We all turned to see a group of four of the bald bloated things eyeing us up and down. Just as one tensed to leap, we opened fire and the first two died in mid flight. The third's head exploded where it stood and the fourth turned and ran.

"Keep tight guys," Flark yelled and I felt bodies hunch up to my sides as we reformed the circle. We remained there for a couple of minutes just looking and listening for any sounds but none came.

"Okay, let's get going shall we?" I suggested. "Keep your eyes and ears open though. Which way do we go? Anyone remember the way from the map?"

"It's a couple of hundred yards that way," Cap replied and pointed to my left. We all looked across the open area of ground. The recreation centre was to our right and the smell of rotting flesh was strong in the rapidly increasing sun.

"Okay, no problem at all," I hissed as I took a deep breath and shouldered my laser rifle. We all felt very vulnerable out here in the open and we were all scared but I wasn't about to admit it to the guys just yet and would happily stay behind and carry on delivering babies to the hairy guys any day, rather than face the creatures out there. We set off briskly in the direction of the Antenna controls; the occasional roars and howls chilling me to the marrow.

Half way there Stitch called out. "Oh my god guys, look." We stopped dead and turned to look at him. He was looking to our left, towards the edge of the area of ground upon which the Island is built. At first I couldn't see anything untoward but then I heard a couple of the guys gasp and Luggs swore.

"What?" My heartbeat quickened as the adrenaline coursed through my veins and panic rose in my chest. "What the fuck is it?"

"Look Sam," Stitch said, his voice now an octave higher than it was a minute ago. "Right down on the ground at the edge of the trench, over there." He pointed and I looked and at first saw nothing but shadows. Then all at once I realised what those shadows were and I almost lost control of my bowels.

"Holy shit on a stick," Luggs whispered and I realised that for the first time since I met him, he was scared and couldn't hide it.

"Oh my good god," Dex said as he wiped a hand across his face and hoisted the Incendipulse gun he was carrying.

"What the fuck is that?" Bud asked as he took a step forward to try to get a better look. Cap pulled him back quickly and yelled for the other two incendipulse guns. Grelly and Luggs hoisted the big flame guns and stepped forward. The black roiling tide of insects poured over the edge of the trench and flowed towards us like an oily river and we stood there, rooted to the spot and unable to look away. This was the stuff nightmares are made of and all those silly vidicoms of folks being eaten alive by millions of insects came swarming back into my mind uninvited.

"Now," Dex yelled and all three opened fire with the Incendipulse guns. A ball of energy shot out of each one and hit the ground right in amongst the black roiling tide. The smell of these weapons is very distinctive and it filled our lungs and made us all gag and cough. As the energy bolts hit, they exploded with the heat of a volcano and everything for several metres around was instantly vapourised. The black tide continued to pour over the edge towards us in a seemingly unending tsunami and time and again the three guys opened fire and incinerated them by the tens of millions. I was just beginning to wonder if we would ever see the end of this tide of insects when the flow pouring up over the edge of the trench rapidly diminished and with two more shots from the Incendipulse guns and it was all over.

We stood, shaking with the adrenaline still coursing through our bodies. After what seemed like several minutes but was probably just a few seconds, I became aware of what sounded like a cough behind me and I turned to see Boy, crying. His hands were grasping at his crotch and I noticed the fresh wet stain down the front of his pants that told us all he'd pissed himself in fright.

"Hey man it's okay now," Baz said as he went to him and put a hand on his shoulder, "they're gone."

"I've never been so shit scared in all my life," Dex admitted as much for Boy's benefit as anything else and we all made sure to heartily agree.

"I'm sorry guys," Boy sniffed and wiped his nose on his sleeve. "I've always been terrified of bugs since I found a huge Tagnoran Beetle in my bed when I was a kid."

"Hey don't apologise," I said. "Back home on Sigma Prime we have this enormous bug called a Catmalone Mantis. They're about a foot long with long pincers that can slice through to your bone without a care in the world and they give me the heeby jeebies and I'm happy to admit it to anyone."

"I got bit by one of those once," Cap said with a grin. "I went to Sigma once for a holiday and saw one crawling across the verandah to our house. Bugs have never bothered me so I went to have a closer look and picked it up."

"What?" I hissed with disbelief. "You picked the thing up? You're an idiot, man."

"Well yeah I know that now Sam," he laughed. "Man did that hurt. It bit right through the bone on my finger, look." He grinned and held up his finger to show us the inch long scar.

I went cold as the image of what must've happened went through my mind. "Yikes," I said as I visibly shivered.

"Okay guys let's get on with it huh?" Flark suggested.

We raced the last hundred yards or so and found the small hut that contained the hatchway that led down to the antenna control box. The antenna itself was intact but bent at an awkward angle. We all stood looking up at it and I motioned for Hank to come and take a closer look.

"Hank, look. What do you think? Is it repairable?"

He gazed up and scratched his head and then nodded. "Yeah, I would say so."

"Okay buddy, you're in charge. Tell us what to do."

"Right ahh, well we ahh."

"C'mon Hank," Dex hissed, "don't flake on us now okay?" Silently I gestured to Dex to calm down. The last thing we needed was to intimidate Hank into forgetting what needed to be done.

"Take your time Hank," I soothed. "We're all here for ya buddy. You tell us what you need and we'll do exactly as you say. This is what you do. It's your bag, you can do this." He nodded and paced up and down scratching his chin and muttering to himself. Finally he looked back up at the antenna and then back at me.

"Okay. We need something to brace the antenna with. It's just like splinting a broken leg in theory. Get it straight again and then I can get the mag receiver and generator nipple realigned. Then it should automatically begin working again."

"Okay guys," I ordered, "we need something to splint the antenna with. Something stiff and strong. Let's take a look around and see what we can find huh? Necessity is the mother of invention so use your initiative. Oh, and three guys stay here with Hank and keep guard okay and yell if anything comes this way." We set off and scouted the area and returned after twenty minutes or so empty handed. "It's no use Hank," I said. "There's nothing around that's strong enough or stiff enough to hold it so it won't move. We need to move to plan B."

"Plan B?" he exclaimed wide eyed.

"Yeah, plan B," I nodded.

"Okay ahh," he began pacing again. "Ahh right then. If we can't fix the one we have then we need a new one. Yeah that's it, we need a new one. A new antenna will do it."

"Where the fuck do we get one of those?" Flark shrugged.

"Anything will do," Hank replied. "So long as it's fairly tall and straight." This wasn't going as well as I hoped and I was beginning to despair when I happened to glance to my right in the direction of the shuttle landing pad. What I saw made me smile.

"How about one of those?" I said. Everyone looked round.

"One of what?" Luggs asked as he came up beside me. "What are you seeing Sam?"

"See where the shuttle pad is?" I asked and he nodded. "Those lights around the perimeter of the landing pad, see em?" I pointed to the dull yellow lights atop twenty foot poles that encircled the landing pad and he grinned.

"Hell yeah, that would do nicely wouldn't it Hank?"

"That would be perfect," he replied with a grin.

"Right, let's go," I said and set off.

"How do we get it out of the ground?" Grelly asked and a couple of the other guys grunted and nodded.

"We shoot it down." I replied. "Everyone aim their rifle at the base of the pole and fire on my mark. Okay guys take aim. And, fire." The air exploded painfully with the noise of nine laser rifles as the base of the nearest pole was sliced clean through. Slowly it began to cant over to one side and fell to the ground, the light at its top smashing to pieces. "Okay, grab hold and let's go," I yelled and made for the pole.

Despite being just a few inches in diameter, the pole was extremely heavy and it took all of us to lift it. We began the shuffle back to the antenna hut, puffing with the weight of our burden. Halfway there a now familiar sound stopped us dead in our tracks. That stomping and grunting meant just one thing; a hunchback was coming to investigate the noise.

"A hunchback is coming," I hissed. "Quick, put it down and stand still. Don't move a muscle." The pole dropped to the ground and we made like statues just as the beast appeared around from the rear of the lab building. It was then that I remembered the guys back at the antenna hut and was pleased to see them all rooted to the spot as we were. The beast stomped towards them, head bobbing from side to side listening for any sounds that might indicate a meal was nearby. Several minutes went by as it circled the antenna hut and at one point got to within a couple of feet of Hank who remained steadfast and didn't flinch. The guys told me later that every single one of them was praying Hank would be safe and I was deeply impressed with his courage and was reminding myself to make sure I told him so, when the unthinkable happened. The beast had just turned to leave the area when Stitch dropped his gun. It landed on the ground with a quiet but audible clonk and the beast snapped its head around in a flash and began stomping right towards him. He was going to be toast in seconds unless we did something, so I shouldered my gun and stepped forward. Before I could start yelling and screaming to get the beast's attention, a loud roar reached our ears, and the beast's too. The stomping stopped as it snapped its head around again and opened it jaws wide, head bobbing frantically as it aimed its lunge. Just then the huge hairy guy Adam stomped up to it and grabbed it around the neck with his left arm, before twisting it around and breaking its neck with his free hand. In less than a minute it was all over and the beast fell to the floor dead. The hairy guy looked at us and then sat down with a thud. We were stunned.

"My god," Cap hissed, "it saved their lives. Did you see that?"

"Holy fuck," I sighed, unable to articulate what I was feeling in a more eloquent way.

"I guess the big guy just earned his place in the team huh?" Luggs said and we all nodded in agreement.

"And he's a he, not an it, okay?" I smiled and the guys all nodded.

We picked up the pole and carried it back and Hank took a look and smiled.

"That'll do nicely," he said. "Now we need to get the other one down. We need to unlock those docking clamps at the base there, then the whole thing will lift out. Then it's just a case of removing the ring clamp that holds the laser generator nipple to the pole, putting it on the new one and lifting the whole thing into the hole and re locking the docking clamps."

"Okay, let's do it," I said as I walked up to take a look.

"The docking clamps are not easy to undo I'm afraid," Hank explained. "This type of setup is usually done with a code locked clamping system to avoid interference or sabotage. Basically what that means is that they need to be unlocked in a certain order or they won't unlock at all.

"Oh shit," Dex exclaimed. "How many thousands of different permutations do we have to go through to find the right one?

"Well only six actually," Hank replied. "Thankfully there are only three docking clamps, which gives us just six possible permutations, so it shouldn't take us long. Okay, now three of you guys, each stand by one of the clamps and when I call your name, you push the button and we'll work out the system that way." Carl, Stitch and Boy stepped up and placed themselves in front of a docking clamp. "Okay ready guys?" All three nodded. "Carl, Stitch, Boy," he ordered and the guys pushed the clamps. Nothing happened. "Okay next try. Carl, Boy, Stitch." Again the three guys pressed their clamps and again nothing happened. "Stitch, Boy, Carl," Hank ordered and once again the guys pressed their clamps. Nothing happened and I swore. "Don't worry," Hank smiled. "Just three permutations to go and one of em has to work. Okay now guys. Stitch, Carl, Boy." The three guys pressed their clamps and we were rewarded with an audible hiss as the gas escaped and the clamps fell away. We cheered and clapped Hank on the back.

"Fantastic job Hank, I'm impressed, really."

"Just basic maths really," he blushed. "Okay now we need to get the old antenna down and remove the generator nipple. Then fix it onto the new pole and lift it into the hole." We approached the antenna and took hold. With a heave we all strained but it didn't move.

"Jeez this is heavier than it looks," Cap remarked. Once again we all strained but nothing happened and we slumped away to catch our breath.

"Once more guys, c'mon," I encouraged and we all strained. Suddenly the pole flew out of the hole and up into the air and we all leapt away in shock. The guys yelled in surprise and I turned to see the hairy guy, Adam holding the pole aloft and looking at me with what can only be described as triumph. The guys all started to laugh and applaud and Adam grunted with what I was sure was pleasure. He put the antenna down and I approached him and looked up into his huge hairy face and enormous grey eyes that shone down at me with wisdom. "Thank you my friend," I smiled and nodded at him. He sighed and grunted at me. "Okay guys let's get that laser off and onto the new pole. "The ring clamp looks like a gas lock clamp." It was simple to remove and I pressed the button in the centre of the clamp that held the generator around the antenna and heard the hiss as the gas escaped and loosened its hold. It fell into my hands and I gave it to Hank, who checked it over and smiled.

"Seems to be fine," he said and I sighed with relief and watched as he fitted it to the top of the new pole.

"Now we need to get this new pole up and into the hole," I said, knowing it was probably beyond our physical capabilities so I approached the hairy guy Adam and smiled. "Can you help us put the new one in?" I asked and indicated to the new pole. Using simple sign language to make it clear what we wanted, I touched the pole and then pointed to the hole and hoped he knew what I was driving at. He stepped over and hoisted the new pole high into the air with one hand and slid it effortlessly into the hole. We clamped the docking clamps in the same permutation as we'd unlocked them and sighed with relief as we clapped each other on the back. With a grin I looked at Adam. "Awesome job, thanks buddy."

"Okay, now we just have to get the generator nipple lined up properly with the mag receiver at the base," Hank said. "I'll get down the hatch and switch the standby on so that when they're lined up, the whole system will automatically switch into operation mode." He lifted the hatch and after a quick check to make sure nothing with teeth was sleeping down there, he descended the ladder and out of sight. A few seconds later a red light appeared from the base of the antenna pad.

"We got a red light here Hank," I called down into the hatch.

"Good," he yelled back. "That means the system recognises that they're not lined up properly. When they are, it'll turn blue so keep a check on that light okay? I'm gonna make tiny movements to the antenna from here and you yell stop when the light turns blue."

"Okay no problem," I yelled back. "Hey guys see that red light? Keep watching it and yell when it turns blue okay?" The guys crowded around the base of the antenna, faces all turned to the floor. "Hey we need someone on lookout. Let's not get sloppy huh." Luggs and Dex shouldered their rifles and kept watch. From down in the hatch, Hank made tiny adjustments to the controls, which made tiny movements to the antenna, back and forth, trying to match up the generator nipple with the mag receiver in the ground so the power could flow once more. Several minutes went by and I began to get anxious. When the guys suddenly gave a yell of "blue, it's blue," it startled me out of my wits. "Stop Hank, it's blue," I yelled down the hatch and Hank grinned back up at me as a low hum could be heard. The hum rose in pitch until it was above the range of our ears and we all cheered and whooped. We were all grinning from ear to ear as I helped Hank out of the hole and closed the hatch. "Awesome job Hank, well done buddy."

"Glad to help," he blushed.

"Well done guys," I smiled as the group gathered around and clapped Hank on the back. "Now let's get back to the lab and wait for my sample to finish. While we're doing that we can decide what we do next."

We made our way back to the lab without incident; the hairy guy Adam following behind us. Once we'd remade the barricade, just in case, I checked around and found a set of doctor's overalls which I handed to Boy.

"Here ya go buddy," I smiled. "You go freshen up huh?"

"Thanks," he blushed.

"It's okay to be scared," I said. "We all get scared sometimes." He smiled and went to the bathroom.

Stitch, Grelly and Cap were at the nutri vend making hot drinks and I went to join Flark and the others at the bag of snacks. "C'mon guys let me in huh. What ya got in there for a big guy like me? Hey what do you reckon Adam and Eve eat?"

"Pretty much the same as us I would assume," Cap replied.

"You think so?"

"Well think about it Sam. They're so much like us in every other way so it stands to reason they'll have a similar diet to us too. Doesn't it?"

"He has a point," Dex remarked and several of the guys nodded.

"Didn't you notice that they never seem to be interested in any of the rotting bodies like the other creatures around here?" Bud remarked. "That would seem to indicate that their diet is a little more sophisticated don't you think?"

"Yeah, good point," Baz nodded.

"Then maybe when we've had a rest up and something to eat, we should go and investigate the stores and see if we can rustle up some real food that they can have too. They saved our lives back there so it's the least we can do huh?"

"Yeah," Luggs replied and several heads nodded in agreement.

Two hours later we sat down in the lab and examined our haul. We'd made the trip to the stores and back and only met one hunchback and three of the fat, bald things, all of which we despatched without a problem.

"Okay what do we have?" I asked as I opened my bag. "I have four large cans of preserved fruit of some kind, 3 bags of dehydrated meat substitute and four of these green things," I said as I held up a green spherical object about nine inches in diameter that looked like it was made up of tightly packed leaves. "It looks like some sort of vegetable don't ya think?" Baz nodded and I heard a grunt behind me and turned to see the hairy guy Adam looking at me and sniffing so I held out the green thing and his eyes widened as he grunted again. He got up and came over and took it from me and bit into it. He seemed to enjoy it so I handed him the other three, which he took and went back to join Eve and the newborn. "Well we have a taker for the green things. What do the rest of you have?"

Between the twelve of us we managed to bring back a decant haul, much of which should be suitable for Adam and Eve. We opened a couple of the cans of fruit and he seemed to enjoy them but he turned his nose up at the small spherical white things about an inch in diameter that Flark brought back. Grelly added some water to some of the dehydrated meat substitute and with a quick zap in the En-Con unit in the kitchen, we were soon enjoying a hot meal of sorts.

"Guys," I said after we finished eating. "We need to decide what we're gonna be doing next."

"How do you mean Sam?" Bud asked.

"Well now we've got the antenna working, we know no more creatures can get onto the island. There may very well still be some hanging around here though. Those flying things for instance; there may be plenty more of those hiding in the various buildings waiting for dark."

"So what are you saying?" Flark asked.

"Well," I replied, "do we have a clean up operation or leave things as they are?"

"How much of the island is there still to explore?" Bud asked.

"There's the hospital that backs onto this lab, the recreation centre, the workshops near the antenna and the accommodation sector. Everything else is clear."

"I vote we leave it as it is," Bud said. "Unless we're planning to use those buildings, in which case we'd have to clear them but if we're not, then it's a waste of energy."

"Anyone disagree with that?" I asked. Nobody spoke as I looked around at the tired group and it was obvious that they were approaching the end of their endurance, at least for today so I was glad that no one disagreed. "Okay then let's leave things as they are, at least for now and if anything changes or we find ourselves under siege, then we rethink okay?" Everyone nodded so we settled down to wait for my sample to finish processing. We chatted and got to know each other and by the time the buzzer let me know my sample was done, several of the guys had dozed off.

The floor in the lab was hard and I rubbed my numb backside to get the blood flowing again as I sauntered over to the processor and pressed the screen for a digital readout. What greeted my eyes shocked me rigid. "Holy fuck," I exclaimed and pressed the screen again to ensure the information was uploaded to my own mobile sampler.

"What's up?" Flark called from behind me.

With wide eyes I turned and looked at the group, the astonishment still clear on my face. "I know who our mystery slasher is."

CHAPTER NINE

The room went silent and eleven faces looked at me expectantly, eyes wide and mouths open. They stared at me and I stared back, the knowledge I'd just gained stunning me into silence for a moment. This was the last thing I'd expected.

"Well?" Luggs said as he held out both hands and shrugged.

"Sam, come on man, the suspense is killing me," Dex encouraged.

"It's the kid," I whispered, unable to believe it myself and not surprised when they didn't either. "The kid did it."

"What?" Flark exclaimed as he looked around at the other guys. "The deaf and dumb kid? No, no I'm sorry Sam but that has to be a mistake." The other guys all nodded at him.

"The sample is confirmed as Agrillian blood type 5340QA with clone marker reference P84MJ756, belonging to Edward Kitt." I showed them my sampler readout so they wouldn't think I was making it up.

"But I thought the old guy was Kitt," Cap said. "Kitt Frail and his grandson Eddy Frail."

"Well it's not such a departure is it?" I replied. "Kitt Frail, Eddy Frail, Edward Kitt; come on guys even I can work that out."

"But he's just a kid," Luggs said. "How old is he? Nine or ten maybe?"

"Old enough for puberty to have hit," Baz replied and I nodded.

"Y'know it could be the old guy and not the kid," Carl said. "We're just assuming it's the kid because we know him as Eddy but if they've changed their names around, the old guy could be the Edward."

"And they've probably taken names down through the family," Baz said. "It's Agrillian tradition that male names continue through the generations and they will most likely have done the same."

"So until we know for sure, we have to put them both into restraints until I can take a sample from each of them and see which matches this one. Baz, you said the clones had a mark branded on the backs of their necks?" He nodded in reply. "What sort of mark is it?"

"The ones that were deemed healthy were given a brand yeah but the ones that were euthanased obviously didn't have it. It's a barcode with a unique number that identifies each one. If one of the crazies escaped the euthanasia they wouldn't have the brand and as the kid was obviously born within the last ten or twelve years he won't have it. Remember all this happened a couple of hundred years ago and all the clones should've died out long ago so these two are obviously descendents of ones that escaped somewhere. The only way the brand is gonna help you is if the killer is one of the safe ones who carries it, which is unlikely as he doesn't look old enough to come from way back then. They have normal life spans like the rest of us so those original ones shouldn't be alive now. He would have to be nearly two hundred years old."

"But they're clones," Boy remarked and we all looked round at him and frowned. "They're identical to their parent and therefore their blood will be identical too won't it? That record you have could very well be from a couple of clone generations ago but that doesn't matter because our slasher will have identical blood to whoever he was cloned from. It won't matter if he doesn't have the brand."

"But their blood will be unique, don't you see?" Baz remarked and everyone frowned. "If they've been living wild for the past couple of hundred years and interbreeding with each other, the resulting offspring will have different blood to their parents. Remember that it was only the first generation of them that were actually cloned. All of their subsequent generations will be natural conceptions and births like normal folks."

"Then how come the crazy thing has been handed down through their generations?" Carl asked and I nodded furiously. That's what I wanted to know too.

"I heard that the genetic defect in their brains was something that would've always been handed down through their generations," Baz replied, "and that even though subsequent generations wouldn't technically be clones, they'd still have the same defect as the original clone generation, especially as they will have only ever bred with each other."

"Right," I nodded and sighed. This was getting complicated and I ran a hand through my hair, the vague headache making my temples throb, "so we get them both restrained, I get samples from both and we go from there." My next problem was how to secure the pair of them into restraints in a manner that didn't upset the other folks or put them in danger. "Now I need to work out how to get them both restrained safely and quietly without causing a panic amongst the other folks back there."

"Sure thing Sam," Dex replied. "How can we help?"

I was touched that they wanted to help me so readily but I was also aware that it wasn't really their job. What I do can be dangerous; I'm trained and insured against mishaps but these guys weren't. "You don't have to get involved guys. It's not strictly your job and it could be dangerous. I'd hate for any of you to get injured, or worse. You've all seen what he does to his victims."

"Stop being an idiot Sam," Luggs replied. "You can't cope with the two of them on your own, especially as one of them, or even both of them, could be a crazed maniac slasher." The others nodded in agreement.

"I hadn't thought that it could be both of them, but I suppose it could be. It's not beyond the realms of possibility that the other one killed Jena Marks."

"You need the knife Sam," Stitch replied and everyone agreed that must be a priority."

"He's not just gonna tell us where it is though is he?" Flark said. "How do we find it without spending hours tearing the place apart?"

"He's most likely got it on him," I replied. "They normally do. If it's a one off killing they tend to discard the weapon but if they're committing serial murders, they always keep their weapon to hand. We have to remember that when we restrain him."

"Best idea would be to separate him from the crowd first," Flark said and I nodded. "That way no one else gets hurt."

"Absolutely," I replied. "And thanks guys. For all your help huh? I appreciate it."

"Aww buddy, you wanna hug or something?" Dex said and everyone laughed.

After scouting the hospital next door and ensuring no creatures were lurking there, we dragged two mattresses into the lab and set them down in the corner with pillows and blankets. It was time for us to leave so I went up to the hairy guy Adam and hunkered down and smiled at him. He looked me right in the eyes and grunted softly. As I looked into those eyes I knew we'd made a connection and weird as it sounds, I also knew that if I returned here in a hundred years time and found him still alive, he would recognise me immediately.

"We're gonna leave you in peace now buddy. Thank you for your help. We thought you might want to be a little more comfortable," I said as I indicated the mattresses. He looked at me for several moments before giving another soft grunt and I knew he'd understood me. Then I gazed down at Eve, cradling the newborn Floxy to her breast and smiled. "Your daughter is beautiful."

"Aww look at her," Luggs said and I turned to see all the guys had crept up behind me and were looking at the baby.

"Ain't she the cutest thing you ever saw?" Dex grinned.

"She is indeed," I nodded. "Okay guys let's do this. Are all the cans of fruit opened?"

"Yep," Cap nodded. "All the cans of fruit and veggies and I put a big bowl of the meat substitute on to soak. They're on the counter top over there."

We left the lab and I felt like I was leaving a friend behind. Closing the main door behind us, we stepped out into the sunshine and listened. It was so quiet it was spooky and I involuntarily shivered. We'd become so used to the howls and screeches that the quiet was very unsettling. We all agreed that getting the laser net working was a really great idea and we felt a lot safer as we made our way back than we had on the way out the day before. We walked down the path towards the recreation centre and I wondered again how many creatures were still hiding within the remaining unsearched buildings, one of which was directly in front of us. We made our way along the windowless wall of the recreation centre and saw the cell wings ahead, the bodies piled up and stinking now. As we stepped out from the shelter of the recreation centre, a crash from inside brought us all to a stop. We hugged the wall and I looked at my companions.

"Do we investigate and deal with it or do we leave it and make a run for it? Majority vote wins." Everyone looked at each other and Luggs swore.

"Shit. Okay come on," he said and stepped towards the still open main door.

Five minutes later we hauled the bodies of four of the fat bald things outside and shut the main door. An investigation of the building brought the discovery of a large supply of beer which the guys were very happy to find.

Bud was was checking out the merchandise when he saw the hatchway in the floor and called out. "Hey guys come and look at this."

"That'll be the cellar," Boy said, "where they keep their stock. It'll be cold down there so they keep it there to keep it cool. Laying on my belly, I pressed my ear to the hatch and listened for anything that might indicate something was hiding out down there. Silence greeted my ear so I gingerly lifted the hatch and peered down into total blackness.

"Okay so who's first?" I hissed, partially as a joke but partially because I didn't fancy doing it myself. No one laughed.

"Hey it was your idea buddy," Dex said. "After you." This time I did hear a giggle or two; me and my big mouth huh? Taking a deep breath, I slowly reached down with a foot and felt the top of the set of steps. With a last look at the guys I took another tentative step down. As I took the third step down the blackness began to stifle me and I recognised the beginnings of panic. A split second before I lost my nerve the blackness below me suddenly exploded into light and I gave a yelp of surprise, which was met with guffaws of laughter from up above. My heart leapt in my chest and I looked up to see Luggs crying with laughter, hands on his knees and his body shaking with the effort.

"Great job guys," I grinned. "Nice."

"Hey man you should've heard yourself," Baz replied through his laughter. "Yelled like a schoolgirl ya did."

"I did not," I replied as I hopped down the last few steps and then suddenly gave a howl of distress and threw myself headlong out of sight of the open hatch. It was difficult not to laugh as I dove for the cover of a stack of boxes and lay face down so that just my lower legs stuck out and tried to be quiet.

"Sam?" I heard a voice that sounded like either Boy or Bud call out.

"He's shitting us," Carl laughed.

"Nice one Sam," Dex yelled. "Bring us a beer would ya?" My chest heaved with the effort of containing my laughter but I stayed put and listened. "Sam? Come on Sam this isn't funny buddy."

"If you're fucking with us I'm gonna kick your ass," Luggs grunted. Then I heard footsteps and suddenly hands wrapped themselves around my ankles and pulled.

"Hi guys," I grinned. "Who's the schoolgirl now huh?"

A search of the cellar revealed a huge stock of booze of all different types and we helped ourselves to a beer apiece to wet Floxy's head and celebrate Hank's genius that got the antenna working again.

"Okay, this is what we'll do guys," I said. "When we get back to the Admin block, I'll stay outside with Dex and Luggs and the rest of you go inside. Tell them the three of us were lost to the creatures. You then tell them the laser net is working again and that the stores are chock full of food and you ask Kitt if maybe him and Eddy wouldn't mind coming along to help shift some of it so everyone can have some decent food. When you get them outside, I'll despatch Kitt with a tranquiliser dart. He'll be out for hours so we can get him restrained somewhere and I can test a sample of his DNA with the sample I took from the overalls and see if they match. If they match, then he's at least one of our guys and he stays under guard. Then I test the kid and see if he's related to my sample as well."

"Sounds fine to me," Cap replied and the others nodded.

"Okay, let's do it," I said and made for the stairs.

The afternoon shadows were getting long as we made our way around to the front of the Admin block. Dex, Luggs and I hid ourselves behind the entrance porch that jutted out from the main door. We watched Flark as he and the others shoved open the door and disappeared inside. Their footsteps got fainter as I retrieved my tranquiliser gun that I had prepared before we left the recreation centre and waited. The sound of footsteps from within brought me out of my musings and I nodded to Dex and Luggs. We melted back into the wall as much as we could as we heard the main door open with the faintest of squeaks.

"I really appreciate this Kitt," Flark was saying, "and everyone will be delighted to have some proper food again."

"No problem at all," Kitt replied. "Eddy and me are happy to pull our weight."

They stepped into view and began to walk towards the stores, their backs to us. With practiced silence I crept forward and Kitt was unconscious before he knew he'd been had. He fell to the floor and Eddy went nuts. Boy held his hand and tried to soothe him as I took out my mobile sampler and got some of Kitt's DNA.

"It's a match," I said as I stood up. "Kitt's DNA matches that I found on the blood stained overalls hidden in the air vent. Now the laser net is up and working we can install him downstairs in one of the cells before he wakes up and then I'll test Eddy. Good job guys, thanks for all your help."

"My pleasure Sam," Luggs said as he spat at Kitt. "I just wish you'd go on inside for a moment and leave me in charge of this psycho fuck kiddy killer."

"I know buddy," I replied "but then you'd be in one whole mess of trouble and he ain't worth that." He was still glaring at the unconscious Kitt as I put a hand on his arm to emphasise the point and he gave a deep sigh.

"There's something you should know Sam," Boy said. I turned and looked and saw a grave expression on his face and behind him, Stitch, Hank and Flark all looked at the floor and I knew right off there'd been another murder while we'd been gone.

"Oh no," I replied and wiped a hand through my hair. "There's been another one, yes?"

"Two more," Hank said quietly. My blood left me and I went cold as I took in his words.

"What? Two? Shit."

"One of em was getting out of this place in a month." Grelly said. "His time was up and he had a family who had waited for him and a job to go back to. He was gonna have a chance to have a good life again and now he's dead."

"Where are the bodies?"

"Wrapped in table cloths just inside the door here, near Meesha, Jena and Ronjo's bodies."

"Throats cut, like the others?"

"Yep."

"We need the knife guys," I said. "Is it on him Luggs?"

"Nope."

"Dammit," I hissed. We really needed to find it but I knew we had a slim chance of finding a knife in a huge place like this and my heart sank. "We'll just have to hope he decides to tell us when he wakes up cos I don't fancy our chances of finding it in this place do you?"

"Well we found the overalls," Grelly cut in. "There are a lot of guys in here and I can tell you now every one of em will be more than willing to tear this place apart to find it."

"We'll draw up a plan of action like we did when we searched for the overalls," I said. "We divide the place up into small sections and get each team to pick the place apart methodically from the bottom up." The guys nodded and that lifted my spirits a little. It was handy having so many willing helpers on this job; I knew I wouldn't have been able to do this alone and I was grateful. "Okay let's get this asshole down in a cell and then I'll get a sample from Eddy. Then we go tell the troops huh?"

Dex and Luggs grabbed Kitt by the arms and hauled him up. Boy was still struggling with Eddy so I held the door open and they dragged him through and headed for cell wing four. Grelly came with us and showed us how to operate the laser fences on the cells so Kitt could be secured without us having to worry about him escaping and we left him in a cell to sleep it off. As we headed up the stairs we heard the scream that rooted us to the spot. We looked at each other open mouthed, then as one we raced up the stairs and back into the main entrance hall. A man lay on his back and at first all we could see was the soles of his boots that twitched every couple of seconds. A second, much smaller body sat astride him, his back to us and seemed to be struggling with something out of our sight. As we slowly moved to our right, the man's left hand came into view and that too was twitching in time with his feet. We were mesmerised at the sight and although we all knew that something was terribly, horribly wrong, we were powerless to act and slowly made our way around to get a better view.

The floor for several yards around was wet with blood but instead of a gently spreading slick like in the vidicom movies we all watch from time to time, we saw angry sprays several feet long in all directions; one of which had hit the wall and reminded me of some of the offensively overpriced modern artwork I'd seen on my travels. Eventually we'd moved around enough to recognise the body as Boy, lying flat on his back as Eddy sat astride his chest, struggling to force the large knife through the vertebra. He shoved his weight down on the knife, lifting his backside up from Boy's chest a foot or so and grunting with the effort. Finally he sank back down, exhausted from his failed attempt to behead Boy and turned to face us. He climbed from Boy's body and stood there, soaked in blood from head to toe and just looked at us. His shoe squelched as he took a step towards us before remembering he'd left the knife buried in Boy's neck. He turned back and bent down to retrieve it; having to use both hands to free it from Boy's third and fourth cervical vertebra. He stood and faced us again, the knife held in front and locked eyes with Baz. For a second I was frozen but his sudden scream snapped me out of my torpor. He raced towards Baz and I shot him with a tranquiliser dart. He dropped instantly, the knife skittering across the slick floor and coming to rest at the toe of my left boot.

Once I was able to tear my eyes away I looked down at the knife, transfixed by the sight of it lying there and still trying to get my head around the fact that I'd just seen a kid trying to behead a grown man. Shit, that kind of stuff takes some getting used to and I'll admit I had a few nightmares afterwards over that. Murmurs from nearby brought me out of my trance and I looked up to find a crowd had gathered; brought there by the screams and now they all stood transfixed as we were. Using all of my inner control, I mentally shook the fuzz from my brain and reached into my pocket for my Sterifilm spray. Once my hands were coated I picked up the knife and called for a clean bin liner.

"Get him downstairs and into another cell would ya guys?" A noise caught my attention and I looked up at the crowd to see Marta put a hand over her mouth and make a dash for the bathroom. The blue eyed plank appeared and met my gaze so I nodded towards the bathroom and he ran in after her. "Can we have a couple more table cloths here and some of that cleaning fluid?" While several volunteers cleaned up I bagged the knife, then went up to the first floor and retrieved the overalls from the desk in office thirty seven where I'd hidden them before we left the day before. Now we had our killer, or killers, I could see no need to hide them away. My brain throbbed; I was mentally exhausted as I flopped into a chair beside Nembier.

"Thought you were dog meat Sam," he said quietly. "Your buddies said you and a couple of the others got caught by the creatures out there."

"A necessary subterfuge. Sorry to disappoint you," I grinned.

"Don't apologise to me, I'm glad you're still here. That blue eyed boy is a nice enough guy but I don't really fancy my chances with him in charge of my case."

"I know what you mean," I snickered. "We have the mystery throat slasher now, so you don't have to worry about getting that tagged onto you okay? Thanks by the way."

"What for?"

"For telling me about seeing the guy before. I know you were trying to help but you could've just told me it was Kitt who let you out of the cuffs. It might've ended this sooner and saved a few lives."

"You think so?" he asked me. "You'd have taken my word for it that I saw Kitt and his crazy kid kill my colleagues back home on Agrillia? Really? Look me in the eyes Sam and tell me you'd have believed me. I dare you."

"Point taken," I nodded. "Now how about you tell me all about what happened back on Agrillia huh? This won't be an official interview by the way; that's not my job. You'll have to do that when the relevant authorities take over your custody but I'd sure like to know." He nodded and I sat back and listened as he explained it all to me.

"We'd been working that dig for three months and were making some really interesting discoveries. The site was out in the middle of nowhere and it was great. We were out in the country, doing a job we love with no one around to bug us or order us around. One day we decided to take a day off and go hiking to see the countryside a little. We'd worked flat out since the day we arrived and a day off was just what we needed to refresh our batteries a little. Anyway, we'd been walking for a couple of hours when we came upon a couple of caves and decided to go in and explore. That was our mistake Sam and one I bitterly regret as it was mainly my idea to go in there. I guess I was hoping to find some rock carvings or something and I just couldn't help myself, so I persuaded the other guys to take a few minutes just to look. The first one was empty but the second one was where we bumped into Kitt and his kid. They were asleep and although they could've just been an old guy and his grand kid out camping, we knew this area was not one where campers could usually be found. It's very isolated and they didn't have the sort of gear with them that would identify them as campers anyway and we just knew they were there because they didn't want to be found and it occurred to all of us that they just might be second or third generation illegal clones. There'd always been rumours of clones still living around in the wilds but no one I knew or spoke to had ever actually seen any."

"So what did you do?" I asked.

"We crept away without waking them up. If we had stumbled upon a couple of illegal clones hiding out, knowing what they're capable of, well we wanted out of there fast. We got out okay but one of the guys dropped his wallet and didn't realise until an hour or so later. None of us fancied the idea of going back to get it so we just carried on and decided that when we got back to camp, we'd call in the security force to deal with them. What we didn't realise was that his wallet contained his ID card and the licence for the dig. We effectively gave Kitt and the kid our address and of course, within twenty four hours the two of them paid us a night time visit. As luck would have it, I was up taking a piss when I heard a noise from one of the tents. Something caught my eye in the gloom when I was about to go and investigate and I saw the kid crawl out the back of the tent with a huge knife in his hands. I was scared Sam and you know what? I was too scared to go and help those guys. Instead of going to help my friends I just hid amongst the rocks while they murdered them and waited for them to go away. Have you any idea how that makes me feel? Have you? Those were my buddies Sam. I've worked with them for ten years and they were the only friends I ever had and I stood by and let them be hacked to death cos I was too scared to go and help them."

By the time he'd finished telling me the story, he had tears on his cheeks and I genuinely felt sorry for him. "Thank you for telling me the truth buddy. I'll make sure the authorities know okay?" He nodded and sniffed and I went and got him a drink. Something occurred to me, so I sat back down and turned to face him. "Did you actually see the kid do all the killings or did the pair of them do it?"

"It was just the kid but you know something? I reckon that Kitt only allowed it because he knew we'd found their hideout. It seemed to me like the kid was the actual crazy one."

"How do you know?"

"Kitt was hiding in the shadows and just looked, well, furtive I guess. It's hard to describe but there was just something about him that told me the kid was the crazy one. It seemed to me that they were just doing it to stop themselves being found and the kid euthanased."

"Okay, thanks," I nodded and felt a lot happier now that I had the full story.

Once everyone had found their way back into the canteen and got themselves drinks and sat down, I thought they deserved an explanation so I stood.

"Guys," I called and the room fell silent. "Okay now you all deserve to know what's been going on so here it is. Professor Nembier here gave me information that it was an Agrillian clone who let him out of the restraints the day we arrived and I felt that this was done in order that he be blamed for Jena Marks' murder. When the second murder occurred I knew it couldn't have been Nembier; he didn't have the time. That was when we all knew we had a killer amongst us. When I got the DNA sample from the overalls, I knew I had to get it processed in order that I could at least begin to figure out who it might be. I know we told you we were going to look for some long range comms equipment, but what we were in fact doing, was going to the forensic lab to process my DNA sample. I'm sorry we lied to you but I didn't want the killer to get nervous and put you all in danger while all the best guns were away. I know you lost another two of your friends but if he'd known we were closing in on his identity, we could've returned to find you all dead."

"When they told us you'd died out there we thought we were doomed Sam," one of the inmates called out and several heads nodded in agreement. "We're sure glad you're okay buddy."

"Thanks man. Anyway, when the sample was done and it said it came from an Agrillian clone named Edward Kitt, we all knew it was either the kid or the old guy, or both. We wanted to get them under restraint without any danger to yourselves, and that's why Morry here asked him and the kid to help him fetch stuff from the stores. Me and a couple of the guys were hiding outside and got Kitt restrained so I could get a sample of his DNA, which came back as a match to the overalls. We thought we had our guy but then the kid ups and goes crazy when we were putting Kitt in a cell and Boy was lost. You all saw how he died, it was horrible but I want you all to know that both of them are now downstairs in cells and they can't escape. We also got the laser net working again by the way, thanks to Hank's genius, so no more creatures can gain access to the island. We must be aware however that there may still be more that we haven't flushed out and dealt with yet. All the buildings except for the workshops and the accommodation sector have been searched and cleared, so it's probably wise that no one go wandering around outside without an escort. If you do, you're to blame for anything happens to you okay? So now all we have to do is wait for the liner to return so we can alert the relevant authorities and get off this rock."

"Sir?" a voice called.

"Yeah buddy, what's up?"

"We still have a killer amongst us don't we? What about him?" he said as he nodded towards Nembier.

"Professor Nembier witnessed nine of his friends murdered by Kitt and Eddy back on Agrillia. That's why he went on the run. He was running from Kitt and Eddy and also because he was scared he would be accused of the killings, which he was. I've been doing this job for a very long time and I know guilt when I see it. Professor Nembier is no danger to anyone here but the law states that I have to keep him under restraint until his case can be fully investigated by the proper authorities."

"Okay," the guy nodded and looked at Nembier. "Sorry buddy." Nembier nodded back and blushed.

We spent the rest of the evening relaxing and chatting and by the time we hit the sack I knew I would have no problems sleeping.

CHAPTER TEN

The next morning I awoke feeling pretty good, despite having spent the night on a pile of table cloths on the floor and after a wash down and some breakfast, I decided I'd best take some food and drink down to Kitt and Eddy in the cells. They were both asleep when I approached the cells and I was pleased that I'd had the presence of mind to ensure the guys put the kid in a cell three down from Kitt, rather than in one of the ones opposite. I didn't want them communicating and formulating a story between the two of them and with the kid supposedly being deaf and dumb, so long as he couldn't see the old guy, he wouldn't be able to communicate and plot with him. Approaching the first cell I called to Kitt and he awoke immediately and leapt up. Jeez that guy has sharp ears; he was snoring just seconds before and now he was up and alert and ready for anything. No yawning or stretching, not even an early morning fart greeted my presence, just a blank glare.

"Morning Kitt," I said without smiling. "I've brought you both some food and drink, here." His face remained expressionless as I slid his tray into the safety drawer, pressed the button and watched as it slid through into the cell. For a second or two his eyes held mine before he reached in and retrieved the tray and looked at it. "It's not gourmet I'm afraid but you know our circumstances. It'll keep starvation at bay even if you don't enjoy it. We should only have one more day until the liner arrives and we can call for help and you'll be taken into the care of the proper authorities." He didn't respond so I walked down to Eddy's cell and was startled to find him standing right at the front of cell, almost touching the laser fence and glaring right into my eyes. It made me jump the way he was just stood there like that. My heart was still pounding as I walked to the safety tray and he walked with me, matching my movements, glaring at me all the time. This was freaky but I forced myself not to look into his eyes, although knowing he was willing me to gave me the heeby jeebies and almost made me turn and run. As nonchalantly as I could, I pressed the button and watched the tray slide through into the cell and waited to see what he would do. This was the moment when I knew I would have to meet his gaze or he would have the position of power and, well you know me and power games.

With every ounce of strength I possessed, I forced myself to raise my eyes and glared back into his and for several seconds we stood there staring each other down and both wondering who would give in first. It was almost me; so very nearly me but just as I was about to turn away cursing myself, he turned and picked up the tray of food. He then turned away and went and sat down on his bunk and started eating, delicately, daintily, tiny morsel by tiny morsel. It was weird and I walked back to Kitt to find him trying to peer sideways to see what was going on with me and Eddy and I was delighted that he couldn't see. He still held the tray in his hands so I nodded at it.

"Don't let it get cold buddy; it taste's even worse once it's cold." He sighed and went to sit down and began to eat. "I'll come back for the trays in an hour or so. Maybe then you might wanna talk about things." He still didn't respond so I started to walk away but before I got halfway to the door I heard a crash followed by the sound of sobbing. That was one of those moments when I wasn't sure what to do for the best. Should I immediately go back and talk to the guy or should I continue walking and let him mull things over for a while? He made my decision for me by calling my name so I turned and headed back to the cell. He was sat on his bunk, head in his hands and the tray on the floor. For a moment I stood and watched him sobbing, not knowing quite what to say. The guy's a murderer but a part of me felt sorry for him. I know, call me a crazy dumb fuck but hey, I have a heart y'know.

"I'm sorry for everything Sam," he said between sobs. "Believe me I never wanted to get into this mess but once things started happening I couldn't get out of it."

"Start from the beginning," I sighed. "This isn't an official interview by the way, that's not my job but I want to understand it."

"Do you know about the Agrillian Outbreak?" he asked and I nodded. "When the outbreak happened, my grandfather, who was also a clone, was ostracised from the community he'd lived in all of his life. Despite being healthy and no danger to anyone, the neighbours made his life a misery. One day they cornered his wife and beat her nearly to death. She was a clone too and had just given birth to my father. They both left the community that night and went deep into the countryside and lived wild with their newborn. Pretty soon they met a few other runaway clones, all of them healthy and no danger and they formed their own secret community right out in the wilds where no one could ever find them. My father grew up and took one of the clone girls as his wife and they had a son, me. In turn, I grew up and married too and had a daughter and she too, took a husband from our secret community and they quickly had a child. That child was healthy and fine as a kid but when he hit puberty we quickly noticed things that told us he was the first one born into our community who was bad."

"So why didn't you?" I left the question unfinished and he looked up at me and sighed.

"Why didn't we kill him? he asked and I nodded. "We were going to. We had a community meeting and discussed it and it was agreed that he should be killed for the good of us all and the greater Agrillian community. We told him we were going for a picnic by the river and he seemed to accept that but along the way we met some hikers and one of them went to hug him and it set him off. That's what does it for him by the way Sam, hugging is his trigger. Every one of the bad clones had a particular trigger that would set them off. It could be anything; a word or even having certain colour hair. For Eddy it was hugging and one of those hikers went to hug him and he took her own knife from her belt and cut her throat."

"Shit," I replied as I ran a hand through my hair. "Just a hug is what starts it for him? That's what sets him off?" He nodded. "But it's so natural for people to want to hug a kid."

"I know and that's why I've always tried to keep him slightly apart from people and why I never encourage anyone to get close to him or try to engage him."

"What happened with the hikers then? Why didn't you kill him like you planned?"

"The other hikers went nuts and ran off. We knew we were in trouble so we had to leave and go on the run. My daughter was terrified and she started to cry and forgot herself and put her arm around Eddy. He still had the knife from the hiker woman and he used it to kill his mother, my daughter. I was grief stricken at losing my daughter and I just couldn't kill my grandson too right there and then, so I took him and we ran. He was my only link with my daughter you see."

"I understand that but it was too much of a risk."

"I know and I always knew I would have to kill him sooner or later. We took to living in a cave we found and everything was okay until that man left his wallet behind and we knew we'd been discovered. There was no choice but to either give ourselves up or deal with the guy and move on again. I know what I should've done but have you any idea how hard it is to make the decision to give yourself willingly to certain death? We may be clone descendants Sam but our survival instinct is the equal of anyone else's and I know it was a failing but I wanted to live. I'd never harmed anyone in my life."

"And of course if you had killed Eddy and he'd been found, you'd then be accused of being one of the crazies and would be euthanased yourself," I said and he nodded.

"Exactly. It was a no win situation for me. Anyway we went to the camp where the workers were and it was the first time I actually instructed him to kill. I tried to do it myself but you know what? I didn't even have the guts to do it myself so I told my grandson to do it and watched as he went from tent to tent. It was as I watched that I knew I had to deal with Eddy, so I changed our names and left Agrillia on the Sally B. I knew the liner called at Floxham so I told them I was visiting a relative here and booked a place on the shuttle. I intended to give us both up when we got here."

"So why did you free Nembier?"

"I heard him telling you that he was from the scientist's camp and that he was accused of the murders, so I set him free and hoped he would escape and manage to evade capture. It was the only way I could think of to try and make up for what we'd done. I didn't want him to be executed for Eddy's crimes. It was while I was setting him free that Eddy killed Jena Marks. She must've put her arms around him or snuggled up to him or something. I'm so sorry for everything." His face crumpled and he slumped to the floor and sobbed.

"So how come I got a DNA sample from the overalls?" I asked him. "They're way too big for Eddy to wear and when the sample came back as belonging to Edward Kitt, we all assumed it was you and that you'd changed your names."

"He did wear them. He sometimes wets himself overnight and I'd given him the overalls after he had an accident," he explained. "Later the same night I got him up and told him to take a pee and I guess Mr Tyle was there and must've put an arm around him or something. Eddy was covered in blood so I got him a clean pair and hid the dirty ones."

"Is it just coincidence that all the victims are Agrillian?"

"No it isn't a coincidence. All of us who are descended from clones have a strange ability to know when we're in the company of another Agrillian. I don't know why and the fact hasn't been documented because we haven't spoken much about it. Maybe it's because of our clone heritage that we can recognise others who share our DNA, I don't know but all of the umm, bad clones only ever attacked Agrillians. My grandfather used to tell us of a guy he worked with who was from Earth. He married an Agrillian woman whose uncle was a clone. He'd married another clone and had three kids who were all fine and healthy. Two of them married clones and had children and one of them turned out bad. They were having a family celebration one day when the Uncle's grandson went crazy and slaughtered them all with his Uncle's laser rifle he kept for hunting. The only ones who were spared were the Earth guy and his mixed race daughter he'd had with his Agrillian wife."

"I wonder why that should be." This news was both intriguing and unbelievable.

"Even we don't know. Maybe it's divine retribution for interfering with nature," he replied with a shrug. "That was another reason I wanted to get Eddy away from Agrillia. The likelihood of us meeting other Agrillians would be much less and there would be more chance of me getting him here without anyone else being harmed."

"And what about your names?" I asked. "Are you really Kitt Frail?"

"No I'm Frank Kitt and he's Edward Kitt. I changed my name but he won't answer to anything but Eddy so I had no choice but to risk it with him and I gave us my mother's name of Frail."

"And is he really deaf and mute?"

"Yes he is," he nodded. "A lot of the clones had other physical deformities and disabilities and it's something that's always been passed down through our generations. It's part of the cost of cloning I guess."

"I wish I could tell you everything will be all right," I told him, "but I can't. They can surely do tests though to determine whether you are one of the umm, bad ones or not, so once they find out Eddy is the one you may avoid the death penalty. Just be honest with them and tell them everything, like you just told me huh? I can't make promises but from what you told me, you're not without hope. They'll take your family loyalties into consideration. They're not unfeeling robots buddy okay? Now, do you want some more food?"

"Yes please," he sniffed. "Thank you for listening and not judging."

"Hey, many folks call me a Merc, which I'm not but I am a good guy sometimes. I do have some redeeming features y'know." It was like a weight off my shoulders now that I knew the story and I was smiling as I returned to the canteen to get him more food. Baz was there eating breakfast. "Hey buddy, sleep okay?"

"Not bad thanks," he said between mouthfuls. "Yourself?"

"Yeah like a log for once."

"It's great how finally getting a mystery slasher finally behind bars can affect one's sleep huh?

"It sure is," I snickered.

"Oh by the way. Morry and Chip have gone out to the shuttle to check the comms for a signal from the liner; it should be within range now and should get here sometime today or late tonight."

"They went by themselves?" I exclaimed.

"Hell no, they took Luggs and Dex with em just in case."

"Okay thanks. I'm looking forward to getting away from here."

"I'll bet you are. They said that if they get in touch with the liner, they're gonna get the word out to the authorities so this place can be cleaned up and sorted out by the proper people."

"Good," I nodded. "Y'know I've been thinking about that and something occurred to me. If the liner comes back today, or even tomorrow and picks us up, you guys are gonna be stuck here by yourselves until help gets here. I don't like that Baz; I don't like it at all."

"Aww we'll be okay now the laser net is working again. Don't worry about us Sam."

"Anything could happen and who knows how long it'll take for help to get here? I'm gonna think on it for a while. I just have to take Kitt some breakfast."

Flark and the blue eyed plank returned with Luggs and Dex and all were smiling so I guessed they'd got some good news for us.

"We are now within range of the Sally B," Flark grinned, "so we told them everything that's happened here and asked them to call for an emergency team to get here as quickly as possible."

"That's great," I nodded. "Any idea how long that's likely to take?"

"Well," he said as he scratched his chin. "The Sally B should be here before nightfall and they've asked me to send back everyone from the liner. They will then return in the shuttle with the liner's security team to help out here until the emergency team arrives."

"Well I have to stay here with Nembier, Kitt, and Eddy until someone from the relevant authorities can take over responsibility for them. I have to see the process through or Nembier won't get a fair trial and Kitt and Eddy could get away on a technicality if I don't do my job properly."

"Captain," Dex said. "I'd like to stay and help if that's okay. I'm useful here and I want to help."

"Me too," Luggs cut in. "If that's okay Captain."

"And me," Cap nodded.

"I agree guys," Flark replied. "We're the best guns here and the Sally B's security team isn't trained for this shit. They're bouncers not soldiers. Chip, I'll send you back with Marta and the bodies of Meesha, Jena and Ronjo. The rest of us are gonna hold out here. These guys here need us, especially as we don't know what's lurking in the accommodation sector and if the laser net should go down again, or if Kitt and Eddy get free and go on the rampage, they'll be toast."

"So we just have to wait for nightfall and then we'll have some more muscle down here," I said and Flark nodded. "Maybe they can help us build a few bonfires?"

"I was wondering whether we should do something," Luggs said. "The stink is beginning to creep inside here now."

"And it's dangerous," Dex added. "There'll be germs and stuff. We could get sick."

"Yeah," I nodded. This had been bothering me ever since we arrived actually but I hadn't said anything because I wasn't sure what to do. On the one hand it seems a little unfeeling to just burn all those bodies without some kind of proper service. They're people after all; husbands, wives, mothers, fathers, sons y'know? On the other hand the stink was getting unbearable and I was thinking about disease too and that's a real danger. We don't want to be stuck here with over four hundred sick people all shitting and puking everywhere. "We have to deal with it and when the other guys get down here, I reckon it should be our first job in the morning."

"Agreed," Flark nodded. "When we go to check the comms later on this afternoon, I'll relay these decisions to Captain Hann and ask him to send the guys down with suitable gear to help us out."

"And I suppose that if we're gonna be here for a few more days, then we could check out the accommodation sector," Luggs said and Dex nodded. "That'll make the whole island finally clear of the creatures and we could use some comfortable beds and more bathrooms. There's room enough for five hundred in that hotel alone. Everyone could have a proper bed and access to a bathroom. If we have to stay here a few more days, at least we'd be comfortable and I won't have to suffer Dex's armpits."

"There's nothing wrong with my armpits buddy," Dex grinned as he lifted an arm and sniffed, "but your farting is rank." Luggs replied by breaking wind loudly and everyone laughed.

The rest of that day felt a little flat for me. You'd think we would've enjoyed a whole day without having to worry about creatures or mystery slashers but I suppose having spent the past couple of days in such a high stress situation, we all fell a bit flat once we had nothing to do. Some people thrive on stress and others just drift I guess and I'll admit now that as the day wore on, I was looking forward to the big clean up the next day. One thing was playing on my mind though; I wondered what I should do about Nembier. He was still in custody but having to keep a watch team on him twenty four hours a day was a drag, for him as well as us so I asked him if he'd rather go into a cell down below or remain here with a watch team.

"It's up to you," I said. "If you'd rather stay as you are then you can stay here. If you'd rather be in a cell then you can have that. It's your choice buddy, I'm not gonna force it on you."

"I'd like to stay here if that's okay but maybe take the cell during the night? A bed to sleep in would be real nice, the floor in here is mighty hard and I'm not a young man anymore."

"Sure thing," I nodded. "No problem at all." The watch team guys were happy with it too as it meant they wouldn't have to stay up all night anymore so everyone was happy. At the end of the day, even if Nembier did escape, where the fuck is he gonna go? We spent the rest of the day doing something I'm almost embarrassed to admit to but it was fun. We put on an impromptu concert and anyone who had any kind of an entertaining talent got up and did a turn. It was amazing to see the variety of talent we had too, from singers and dancers to magicians, poets and one huge guy stripped down to his underwear and gave us the most awesome show of the whole day. He stood on his hands, on one hand, balanced on his head and spun around and twisted his body around while only balancing on his hands; it was awesome. There was one guy who was a terrible comedian and had us laughing so hard we cried because he was so bad. Another guy acted parts from famous vidicom movies, only he kept getting the lines wrong and it was funnier than the comedian's jokes. We then did this story thing that someone suggested and at first I groaned but actually it turned out to be fun and had us all using our brains as well as our creativity. One guy started off by making up the first few lines of a story, then the next guy carried the story on for another few lines, then a third guy carried on and so on. When the time came for the group to head out to the shuttle I knew some real connections had been made between folks and I was sure some friendships made during that experience would last for years to come and it pleased me to know that something really good could come from something so awful.

"Okay guys," Flark announced. "It's time we got out to the shuttle. Can we have some volunteers to carry Meesha, Jena and Ronjo's bodies? A hundred guys stood immediately and I smiled as I realised just how deep those connections we'd all made during the past couple of days had gone. The blue eyed plank and Marta said their goodbyes and she even gave me a kiss on the cheek and made me blush. I shook hands with Chip and realised he probably didn't deserve the nickname I'd given him.

"I haven't been much help around here Sam," he smiled, "but I want to thank you for everything you've done."

"Hey you did your bit buddy," I replied truthfully. "You kept the place going while we were away at the lab and no one has complained about how you ran things. Not to me anyway. I'll buy you a drink when I get back up there okay?"

We set off to the shuttle to see Chip, Marta and the bodies of Meesha, Jena and Ronjo back to the liner and to wait for the security guys to arrive. The journey went without incident and we loaded the bodies onto the shuttle and watched as it lifted off and into the sky. We expected it to return in around an hour, so we settled down to wait it out. Suddenly we all heard a crash from one of the stores buildings a hundred yards to our left and all guns were immediately alert. Another crash, followed by a thud and then the hairy guy Adam appeared with Eve and the newborn Floxy, their arms laden with food. Dex laughed and everyone lowered their guns, whilst the volunteers who'd carried the bodies and not met him before, exclaimed in shock. The three saw us and Adam grunted in that way I'd come to think of as recognition, so I raised a hand and smiled at him and they approached us cautiously.

"Hey buddy, how are ya huh?" I smiled and he grunted quietly in response. It was good to see them both healthy and happy and I smiled as I looked at Eve. "You're looking fully recovered now hunny; I'm glad to see you up and around and fit again." Finally I looked at little Floxy and despite myself, my heart gave a little flip and I couldn't help but grin. "Aww she's gorgeous," I said as I stood on tiptoe trying to see her as she snuggled into Eve's chest. Without warning Eve walked towards me until she was just a couple of feet in front of me. She reached out and let her hand come to rest on my shoulder and man that choked me up. Not able to resist, I touched little Floxy and she wriggled and yawned. "Hello beautiful," I said as I tickled her chin.

"Hello papa," Luggs said from behind me in a squeaky high pitched voice that sent everyone off into guffaws of laughter.

Adam grunted softly and looked into my eyes and something passed between us. A moment that I can't really describe adequately but it was almost as if he was saying, "well buddy, maybe we're not so ashamed of how you've evolved after all," and I was really happy to know that. Goose pimples rose on my arms as I looked into his huge grey eyes and again saw myself looking back at me, but this time what stared back at me was a friend. The pair and their newborn wandered off and I went back to endure the taunts of the guys while we waited for the shuttle to return.

The shuttle arrived and fifteen hefty security guys with protective bio hazard suits, breather units and laser rifles joined us. They unloaded crates of spare suits, breather units and cremblocks, which would ensure the bodies burned quickly at a high temperature. By this time the afternoon shadows were lengthening so we made our way smartly back to the Admin block. On the way the guys got their first look at the task that awaited them in the morning and all were more than a little shocked at the number and state of the bodies. A couple vomited on the way, due to the smell and I groaned inwardly and shot a look at Dex who rolled his eyes and shook his head in response. Luggs tried to suppress a grin and almost triumphed. While the new arrivals were settling in and getting themselves a drink and something to eat, I went to the cells to check on Kitt and Eddy.

"You okay Kitt?" I asked as I approached the cell to find him doing press ups on the floor.

"Apart from bored out of my skull yeah," he replied and stood up, breathing hard.

"Sorry about that," I shrugged. I didn't quite know how to reply; I felt sorry for him being locked up all the time and I know I'd go out of my brain if I lost my freedom.

"It's not for you to apologise Sam," he sighed and sat on his bunk. "It's just that there's absolutely nothing to do and no one to talk to. Could you perhaps try and find a vidicom unit somewhere. There must be something in one of the offices."

"We're going to check out the accommodation sector tomorrow, just to make sure there are no creatures lurking there so if I come across any I'll bring you one."

"Thank you, that would make it more bearable."

"No problem. Now I'll rustle you both up some food and get you some clean overalls so you can have a wash and change okay? Oh by the way, Nembier will be spending the night in a cell too so you'll have someone to talk to at least until he falls asleep."

"He is?" Kitt frowned.

"Yeah, I gave him the choice and he said he'd like a bed rather than the floor for the night time so he'll be spending the nights down here with you. Is that a problem?"

"No, not at all."

"Okay great. Oh, and umm, now the laser net is up and working again, the security vidicom in here is working now too so everything you all say and do is being recorded okay? It's my duty to tell you that and I'm sorry I forgot when you first came down here." He nodded and I returned to the canteen and arranged for food and a change of clothes for them both and instructed the guys who volunteered to take it down, that on no circumstances were they to approach the cells other than by the safety drawers. Being seasoned inmates themselves they didn't need telling twice. It was a surprise to me that Nembier had opted for a cell at night and I wondered if he would be okay with sharing the cell block with Kitt and Eddy but he was fine about it and even expressed the desire to talk to Kitt to try and understand why everything happened the way it did. He was after some sort of personal closure I guess and I can't blame the guy; I wanted to understand the whole thing too. That's why I asked Kitt to explain so I can't blame Nembier for wanting to know. When folks started drifting off to their chosen sleeping places, I escorted Nembier down to the cells and let him pick which one he wanted and to my surprise, he chose the one next door to Kitt. There was an uncomfortable moment of silence as I brought Nembier down and they looked into each other's eyes. Finally Kitt broke the spell by nodding and giving an embarrassed smile. Nembier nodded back and I installed him within the cell.

"Enjoy the bed buddy," I grinned and he nodded.

"Thanks Sam. I'll think of you up there on the floor."

"You do that," I snickered, allowing him his moment of one upmanship. "See you guys at breakfast."

The following morning we were all up bright and early and after a swift breakfast, we handed out protective suits and breathers to volunteers and set out to our dread task. We decided to begin the clean up at the admin and cell wings, as that was where the heaviest concentration of bodies was. Three hours later we had cleared the Admin Block and Cell Wings and everyone was hot and tired. Each pile was laid out with one of the ten inch square cremblocks at its centre. Once the fuse lines were attached Flark stepped forward and said a few words.

"All seeing and all knowing universal creator, we ask that you receive the souls of these, your children and lead them into whatever afterlife you deem appropriate for them. We ask forgiveness for what we have to do here today and we ask that you keep us safe as we wait for help to arrive. Amen." The fuse lines were lit and with a hiss and a whoosh, all the piles of bodies burst into white hot flames.

After a break for something to eat and drink, we decided our next job should be the workshops and the Accommodation sector. We needed to get them cleared before nightfall and it was already approaching mid day. The volunteers who'd helped haul bodies were sent inside and once the security guys had changed out of their protective gear and re armed themselves, we set off. The workshops were clear so we headed over to the Accommodation Sector. This part of the island consists of ten shared houses for staff and five hundred visitors and other guests in the hotel. We'd found out from the plans that the hotel rooms were a mixture of singles, doubles and family rooms totalling two hundred and ninety four rooms on five floors to be checked for creatures and bodies. We were dreading this job and all of us remembered our first harrowing experience the night we got here and had to clear the Admin Block to make it safe for us. A lump formed in my throat as I remembered clearing the cell wings and how Ronjo lost his life saving me. This was the last thing I wanted to do again but it was necessary so I shook my head and rolled my shoulders around.

"Okay people, let's do it."

Amazingly, the Accommodation sector's ten shared staff houses yielded just a dozen bodies and three of the flying creatures. The hotel was clear of bodies and creatures and we actually found a dozen or so people alive and hiding out there, all of whom were terrified at the sight of us and thought we were escaped inmates come to murder them. They came at us with shoes, boots and any other personal items they could find to use as a weapon and one brave gal held a hairbrush in front of her and had a look of steely defiance in her eyes that I would be proud to display. We soon had them calmed down and invited them to join the rest of us in the Admin Block and they were overjoyed to accept. We now knew the whole island was clear of creatures and everyone was very relieved. I kept my promise to Kitt and got a spare vidicom from a vacant room in the hotel and took it down to the cell block in triumph. Nembier had asked me to let him stay in the cell for the day so he can Kitt could talk and they were deep in conversation and Kitt had tears streaming down his cheeks so I guessed some closure was going on. They were happy to see the vidicom and were grateful to be able to sit and watch a stream of mediocre movies until they drifted off to sleep.

I was smiling as I made my way back to the canteen and hopped up onto a chair. "Guys? Hey guys," I yelled and the hubbub quietened. "For those newcomers, welcome. I'm Sam Sinclair and I'm a Freelance Law Enforcer, Tag code Sinclair 27593-4/167AZP. I have three prisoners under restraint down in cell wing four, so I'm afraid the cells are out of bounds to everyone without my express permission. During the daytime, one of them will be joining us up here. He's no danger to anyone and is innocent of the crimes he is wanted for but I have to follow the proper procedure and keep him in restraints until I can hand him over to the proper authorities. That doesn't mean he deserves to be treated like an animal okay? He's been through it here with us since we got here and a lot of it while everyone thought him to be a murderer. I don't want to find out he's being bullied while my back is turned. The next thing is that now we know the island is free of creatures, we can continue the clean up tomorrow and should be able to let you all out to get some sunshine by the afternoon. If you do go outside, please be aware that you may see or encounter three large hairy humanoid creatures. They are harmless and friendly and saved our lives a couple of days ago on more than one occasion and if I get even a sniff of anyone being cruel to them, I will go right off top okay?"

"He's only saying that cos he delivered their baby, ain't you papa?" Luggs squeaked and everyone laughed.

I blushed and couldn't help laughing with them. "Okay, okay yeah I helped deliver their newborn and I feel kinda, responsible. Now that we know the island is safe, I vote we all sleep in the Accommodation sector from now on; sleeping on the floor here is getting seriously old. Is everyone okay with that?"

The following morning we cleared the cell wings of the dead, then moved around the island methodically and had the job done by mid afternoon. Everyone was glad to be able to get out into the sun and I escorted Nembier as he took a walk around the island. We could relax for the first time in what seemed like months and some real friendships were made during that experience, many of which I know will remain solid despite the vast distances between them and a few of them, my own. There were a couple of the guys I wanted to keep in touch with and I had already exchanged Unicom numbers with Dex, Luggs and Baz and I knew that we'd all keep in touch and maybe even meet up from time to time. The emergency team finally arrived on the third day after the clean up finished and the day after that, the Law Enforcement Agency arrived to take official control of the prison and I was finally able to hand my prisoners over. Relief flooded through me as I gave them the evidence bags and the data from my mobile blood sampler and data recorder and told them everything Kitt and Nembier had told me and officially signed them over into the care of Floxham's new Governor, who assured me that this new information would most likely ensure Nembier's release. As the shuttle returned for the last of the Sally B's passengers and crew, I went to speak with Nembier for the last time.

"Hey buddy," I smiled and shook the hand he offered me. "You did good Professor. You did good."

"Thank you Sam and thank you for believing in me."

"Just doing my job," I smiled. "I'm sorry again for losing it with you that first day. I've told the Governor all about it, so don't feel it's been brushed under the carpet and if you wish to file a complaint, I want you to know I won't fight it and will happily compensate you okay?"

"You're a good man Sam," he smiled. "Your belief in me in compensation enough. Money I can acquire easily but the belief and trust of another man is a rare treasure and one I wouldn't wish to exchange for money."

"You take care of yourself Professor?"

"Be safe Sam. Be safe in all that you do."

Well, that's where the tale of Floxham Island ends really. We returned to the Sally B and I got some much needed R and R, which the leggy blonde was more than happy to help me with by the way and I was able to enjoy the liner and its delights for four days before my next job came in. Oh, one thing before I sign off. The governor assured me that the three hairy guys, Omega, Adam and Eve and the newborn Floxy would be taken care of and that they and their kind had been welcome members of the Floxham family since the prison was first built. Their scientists study them and learn about them and their medical team take care of their needs. He told me that they'd been trying to encourage them to breed for ages without success and were delighted that they now had a healthy newborn. He also told me he would make sure she was always named Floxy.

Thanks for listening folks; I hope you found my Floxham adventure interesting. Be sure to catch my other video logs huh? This is Sam Sinclair, Tag Code Sinclair 27593-4/167AZP signing off. V-log reference AZ267/M complete.

THE END

COMING SOON

Acts of Life
by Merita King

Jake Elloway has a glittering career as one of Earth's most celebrated vidicom movie stars and enjoys his privileged lifestyle to the full. An arrogant megalomaniac, Jake is handsome and talented, but selfish and indulgent. When he is offered a role that is something of a departure from the muscle bound action heroes he usually plays, he is hesitant to accept. Persuaded by his Personal Assistant to take the role, Jake reluctantly agrees to spend three months living and working aboard an inter galactic freight liner as research for this new role and hopes that his new environment will afford him plenty of beautiful female fans to seduce.

Life aboard the Mayan Queen quickly proves to be anything but comfortable and when the vessel is boarded by pirates intent on kidnapping Jake for a substantial ransom, he realises that not everyone aboard is keen to protect him. When the small group of friends make a desperate bid for freedom, a new nightmare begins.

www.ingramcontent.com/pod-product-compliance
Lightning Source LLC
Chambersburg PA
CBHW071346170626
46811CB00003B/1005